BlackAmber Books

Ma

by the same author

All that Blue, novel

BlackAmber Books 2002

Ma

Gaston-Paul Effa

Translated by
Anne-Marie Glasheen

BlackAmber Books

Published by BlackAmber Books Limited
PO Box 10812, London SW7 4ZG

1 3 5 7 9 10 8 6 4 2

Originally published in France in 1998
under the title *Mâ* by Bernard Grasset

First published in Great Britain in 2002 by
BlackAmber Books Limited

This book is supported by
the French Ministry for Foreign Affairs,
as part of the Burgess programme administered for
the French Embassy in London
by the Institut Français du Royaume-Uni.

This book is supported by
the French Ministry of Culture
(Centre National du Livre).

A CIP record for this book is available from the British Library

Designed and typeset by Peter and Alison Guy
Printed in Finland by WS Bookwell

ISBN 1-901969-09-6

Contents

My life has been naught but a night
where I walked,
eyes wild,
overturning graves.
The time has come
for me to stop
Africa's cry,
to listen to the echo
of flames and skies,
to rise
and look at the sun,
shimmering and superb.

1: The Abduction

▼

Night had fallen and it was already dark in the maze of narrow lanes, on Yaoundé's seven hills, at the ends of the earth, at the ends of the sky ... and there, on the sharp edge of the moon, I, Sabeth, wept.

At the age of fifteen, when night was no different from day, I was still making my way gently through the world. I was a mother, in the depths of a heart not yet deceived by age's mirror. At twenty, tradition stole my firstborn from me. I still remember that last rainy season, the last caress – the blinding prelude to my grief – that put the seal on my obscure union with my son.

It was dusk and the middle of the dry season. The sun, shimmering and superb, was sinking behind the huts as though it had been hooked by the purr of the Sisters of the Holy Spirit's Citroën 2 CV that had just burst into the courtyard. As the car approached, I felt a gnawing anxiety inside me; shock, alarm shut out the peace of the dying day.

My husband was waiting for them, seated at the foot of the palmyra. I remember the curious presence of the French Sisters' car as they made their way across the courtyard. There in the phosphorescent twilight stood the car, the gleam of its bodywork exacerbating my fear, as if death itself were there, as if I could feel it, this death.

My husband had us, my son Douo and me, brought to the courtyard.

I wanted the white Sisters never to reach the house; I wanted to move my husband, sway him, cry mercy.

My only child, my beloved boy, did he sense his father had decided to give him to the nuns, as though the entrusting of our firstborn to the missionaries of the Holy Spirit might encourage him to turn away from idols and embrace the God of redemption?

The Unacceptable flayed the tender happiness in which I dreamed of hiding. From illusion to illusion, I had been led and misled right up until the end. Too late I understood that the drinking of palm wine with the white nun the night before had sealed the contract that would give them my first child.

The bonding, the first five blissful years, the intensity of my relationship with Douo was shattered the moment I revolted against a tradition that demands you give away your firstborn.

Like the owlet moth, I knew what it was to dread the night. The image of Sister Marie-France dragging Douo to the car, the memory of that wrench, which I nurture with a strange and terrifying kind of delight, the constant pain like the yearning that brings back the nightmare of his abduction.

That evening, after they had taken Douo from me, I sat on my pillow. Never again would I hear my son call me Ma with that excess of tenderness to which his love carried him. The sensitive parts of my body spasmed at the distress in the magical syllable he uttered – and all the colours of the world, harsh and forlorn like his cry, suddenly appeared alien.

I continued to concentrate on his face, as though – waking from a dream – I could have embraced him, as though my hands, born and reborn on the child's body, could have held him one last time.

I could see my son's face, and his father's grim face – faces I had studied so often over those five happy years, unaware that love's wounds never heal.

Never would I have believed that the loss of a child could be so painful.

I had seen Douo ill, almost die during a bout of malaria, but for him to be taken from me like that ... I couldn't bear it. The abduction was my cross. I couldn't speak, my nerves were in shreds; I was ready to break like the strings of the kora. Forced to separate from Douo, my soul had been ripped from my body.

For days on end, I sat in silence staring at his collection of grasses, palm nuts, dried hibiscus flowers and empty snail shells, as still, as silent as them, letting myself sink into them before ricocheting to their surface like a stone. The sight of the relics reawakened my longing, like an incessantly recurring pain.

Whispering the echoes of a secret, I knelt, meditated, and slowly calmed down as the first of my tears stained the dust.

The morning of the abduction, I had as usual washed Douo, then, on banana leaves soaked from the water that dripped from him, I had rubbed him with palm oil, stirring tender, deep-rooted sensations, and repeated his name in a last caress.

I had given him the nickname 'Douo' for it touched me deeply and brought me closer to him. Douoooo – like a sigh so full of gentleness – had shown me the depth of my love.

▼

I whispered his name and was filled with joy, the final transfusion from child to mother, from mother to child. I remembered the twin body inside me, as though the small being still dwelt there.

Now that he was alone in Douala, in exile with the nuns, would his heart still beat for years, for days; would it give rhythm to time as it passed?

Stooped over my child's invisible ghost; maimed, shut away in the agony of my own night, I nurtured the devastation within.

Then my faithful companion pain woke up. How attractive he'd grown since Douo had been abducted, eyes dark black, purple black, dark-ringed, trembling with gold flecks. I sank into them, drowned in them as I repeated over and over – Douoooo – two syllables that reverberated like a caress. He haunted me. He knew how we were filled with the places we'd roamed.

I was obsessed with flowers, dried leaves, dragonflies, salamanders captured in the sun, treasures in the dust-covered book of my memory, fossils gathered in a single ruin, images of the child and of dreams and piles of fallen rocks accustomed to mortal wonder. The same day, where nothing happened, started over and over again. Long hot evenings filled with wonder, the veined translucence of a fly multiplying its fleeting bright rosettes, coloured eyes moving, barely visible in the undulating grass, inspired the same adoring expression I had for the child.

I watched a geometer moth fly back and forth from wall to raffia roof. Soon my tear-filled eyes would no longer be able to see it.

Promised a different marriage, I'd felt lost since the day I'd been given to my husband. From furious bitter disappointment to mild rage, I had already suffered a thousand deaths of dereliction.

My nights consisted of fretfulness and anguish, pain and abandonment. Remembering my abducted son, I was she who meditated in asceticism. I'd see angels in habits accompanying the procession that had taken Douo to the convent of the Sisters of the Holy Spirit. God was separating me from my child, tying and untying the bonds between us.

It was as much as I could do to breathe. I was disappearing into my memory like an incarcerated slave. To punish me for thinking of the child I'd lost, my husband's other wives, Emilia and Anaba, gave me all the thankless tasks.

Sometimes, when my thoughts strayed while I was browning a chicken in palm oil or sweeping the yard, I'd feel a shudder of revulsion suddenly stir deep inside; my flesh felt like wisps of thatch or dust retreating into the distance like the sea at the far end of the beach.

▼

I am the only one who remembers Douo nestling against me, and when I do, I am back in the happy haven, bathing in the sun, filled with the ache of bliss. A bird in full flight, the river winding between the rocks, the tingling of the air, the frothy leaves of the banana tree ... This sparkling procession, which breaks up then reforms and blazes briefly, returned day after day to lift me like the ocean waves.

The memory of Douo was like an invisible shard embedded in the most sensitive part of my heart; it suddenly shattered and invaded everything I was experiencing, everything that flayed the fragile past I'd dreamed of hiding in.

The present I banished each time memory returned. In each long, remote, incandescent night, so vast, so pure, the image of Douo flickered like a flare brandished in the distance, like a bush fire breaking out and spreading beneath skies heaving with the cries of children still smelling of the sweet grass in which they'd rolled.

2: Childhood Memories of Obala

▼

Where did my need come from, to submerge myself in childhood memories, to wrap myself in them? It was a way of defying the unacceptable – death, which without warning would surface in me – the feeling that otherwise I wouldn't survive my son's disappearance.

For as long as I can remember, the town of Obala was not much more than the church that told of the town in far-flung areas and which gathered to itself in the middle of a field – like a goatherd his goats – the spiky, red-backed huts around which the River Foulou drew a broken line, thus holding it in a circle as perfectly as a herd of zebus in a pen.

The inhabitants of Obala found it a rather cheerless place, with its winding alleyways and raffia-roofed, mangrove-swamp-mud huts that pulled the shade down over them. Cracked by regular downpours, the walls were crumbling; and as I remember, the alleyways of Obala were very different from those of Yaoundé, eighty kilometres away.

In fact, the alleyways and the church that towered over the market place were even more unreal than my first encounter with my husband.

There were times when I imagined myself crossing the market place and stopping to chat to the stallholders. I couldn't resist the smell of palm nuts, the taste of the *maracuja*, the song of things. And to walk along the road that separated Obala from the capital Yaoundé and come across characters from African mythology, like the wicked panther Zé and the cunning tortoise Koulou, was like a return to childhood.

What I was searching for was the memory of those happy childhood years. I loved the thousand scents that emanated from the Obala countryside, the exquisite jelly of the guava dropped from the tree. In Obala, the air was saturated with the delicate bloom of a silence so nourishing that I always made my way greedily through it, especially on cool evenings during the rainy season when, returning from the fields with my mother and my sister Thècle, I could taste it even better.

In the courtyard of the family home, my father and the village elders would come and warm themselves by the crackling log fire and drink palm wine as they waited, comfortable in the growing heat, for the women to return from the fields and prepare a meal of maize cakes, sorghum cream and groundnut sauce.

After Douo was snatched from me, I felt the need to spend some time in my father's house in Obala. I wanted to escape my dread-filled days. I wanted to get away from my husband, my marriage, my shattered present, to be reminded of a time when I wasn't enslaved, in a place where I wouldn't be afraid of daily life, to return to before my wretched marriage. By remembering my childhood, everything might become possible again.

▼

When at fourteen I made my first trip to Yaoundé, it was to have been the start of something new. I marvel now at these recollections and conjure constellations of images that have no respect for chronology.

In the condensation of dew, the Cameroonian capital is suddenly ablaze with the brilliance of the rising sun, suffused with grace like a vision whose aura – like the one the barn owl makes in a puddle where it flaps its wings – is discernible. A new light materialises, an epiphany in which a star reappears that the eyes perceive once more.

I remember having answered the call to the capital. Yaoundé's three main cafés – La Saladière, Le Cintra, Porter Trente – had been besieged, the cheap eating-places stank of braised meat and stale fat and the pavement cafés were packed. The illegal traders were more arrogant, and pickpockets argued among themselves as to who their next victim would be.

The place was crawling with humanity. It was like emerging from the cold night to come suddenly face to face with the dawn.

Stunning facades dimpled the opposite shore. Seven hills separated me from the sky that looked like tranquil blue milk, a salt-washed shell, the cornea of a staring eye wherein time, whose presence I was unaware of, trembled. The sky inhabits the enigma of the seven hills.

As the light is distilled, peaks and valleys come into view. So many things are sealed. At the top of Mount Fébé, at a height of one thousand metres, there is a clearly defined spot, a narrow entrenchment from which the whole town can be viewed, a precious refuge, a suitable retreat – a place of wonder.

Whoever lives on the hill is the god of the place – Benedictine monks, for example, who go up there to meditate.

It takes forever to climb Mount Fébé – you have to keep stopping. First there's the mango tree with its fragrant fruit, a familiar bird, a ridge path, the grain of a rock. Step by step, I explored the cosmopolitan world, the miracle that made it a garden of revelations. My eye lingered, wandered, travelled the half-wild, half-cultivated, lush earth. I went from one landscape to the next where hills and vegetation glowed brightly.

Walking into the light, I made my way back to the town centre; blinded by the sun, now low on the horizon, I followed the narrow streak of brightness that led me to the central market place. A soft mist filtered the light, the contours of the large buildings blurred and it was difficult to single out the undulating silhouette of the Postal and Telecommunications ministry and the massive skyscraper that was the Bank of the States of Central Africa. The tall facades presented a succession of arches, imposing and beautifully proportioned buildings.

The comings-and-goings of the yellow taxis that jeopardised the lives of the tourists put the finishing touches to the view. What else could I hope to find, and why would there be a place for me in this unempty universe?

Nothing trembled or stirred in this place that suddenly looked like a saturation of space. The town lures, ensnares anything that moves, and captures anyone who passes at the heart of its architectural web.

It gradually dawned on me that Yaoundé had developed by chance, at a time when everything was possible, and that to leave it for somewhere else only happened in dreams. Fleeting moments and places perpetually offered themselves to my hunger, frozen but constantly mutating; light, buildings and landscapes bearing no relation to time, but united under the sign of a common splendour.

3: A Chance Encounter

▼

If, my childhood behind me, I persist thus, with a growing sense of inevitability, it is because I want to see my misfortune through to the end. I seem to be forever attempting to destroy the sacred aura surrounding my childhood memories of Obala, to annihilate all nostalgia for my family home, for the lost paradise I never had.

My mother never initiated me into the ways of a woman's life. And that is perhaps what I was most aware of, as an adolescent – the lack of this apprenticeship. Not once did my mother see me or talk to me as a woman.

It was as if I didn't exist. In the courtyard at night as the sun was going down, she might have said a few words to another member of my family, apparently oblivious to my presence, but she must have known that, had she put her arm around me or spoken one kind word, I would probably have burst into tears, so great was my sense of isolation from humanity.

However, this segregation was something I just wasn't prepared to accept. Rigid with pain, I was hungry for other people. I wanted to matter to them. Not to everyone, but to my mother, or my sister Thècle who would have intuited or recognised the latent passion in me.

All that was needed for this fire, this inner inhabitant of mine, to flourish was the approval or recognition of another woman.

In African families it falls to the husband's wives to ensure that the young women are prepared for the future. I had only one mother and she wasn't interested in me. My mother wasn't ugly but she had a long, inscrutable, somewhat stern face, with a certain hardness around the chin and, like many African women, a haughty or defensive air about her which I think I found intimidating.

When I was twelve I still had a very conventional view of family life, and the fact that my mother had sole responsibility for the running of the house made me see her as a figure of authority. It never crossed my mind that my father might have reproached her for not allowing him to have other wives to relieve her of some of her duties.

My mother might also have given the impression that she ruled the family, that she held it firmly by the reins. All the time I lived with her I don't think I ever suspected that this proud woman actually stood on very shaky ground. Maybe it was because I was too young and too wrapped up in myself, or because I didn't love my mother enough to spare her a thought or show any interest in her as a woman, I never entertained the idea that she might be vulnerable.

I felt I had to defend myself against the ill fortune of being the oldest which, far from helping me fulfil my destiny, threatened to sidetrack me, to pull me into its vertiginous absence; if I allowed myself to be dragged into it, I would never be able to escape. Moreover, because my hunger for life had been unable to find a hold in childhood, I endeavoured to suppress it, out of pique, out of resentment, as much as out of distress.

The hunger returned stronger than ever the moment I left Obala. I had tried to reject life because I so desperately wanted to embrace it and because it had eluded my embrace. I felt lost, made to do loathsome jobs like roasting the pig, digging up brambles in the forest and clearing the undergrowth. But my need hadn't died, quite the contrary, and during that first visit to Yaoundé it made an incredible recovery.

Within sight of Yaoundé, the only approach route to the Cathedral of Notre-Dame contrasted so sharply with Obala's little Marist church that I was instantly filled with the emotion I sought. I would later regret the distraction, the dream.

Outside the cathedral, a stallholder was charging a small fortune for apples imported from France. I was fascinated by the fruit and their indescribable flavour. I think I was expecting them to trigger some kind of emotion in me. I thought the perfect roundness of the apples translated the fruit's natural perfection.

It was then that it happened, the chance encounter that was to turn my life upside down.

As I straightened and opened my parasol to protect myself from the strength of the last rays of the setting sun, I struck the stranger standing next to me in the face.

A look of indescribable anger and rage spread across the man's face, and in what seemed like an eternity, he fell backwards, causing his surprisingly fleshy backside to crash down with a spirited, sinewy ripple.

I don't know how, but I knew – more surely than if my worst enemy had stuck pins in a voodoo doll – that the unexpected undulation of the man whose wrath I could feel had brought misfortune crashing down on me.

When the stranger stood up, without so much as a twitch of his facial muscles, he glared threateningly out of the corner of his black eye. Then, in an attempt to express the extent of his fury, he glowered as fiercely as he could from the shadowy part of his pupil. Then he ranted and raved – the dark eyes of his frosty face ablaze with hatred – and finally demanded that I minister to him on the spot.

There in front of the French apples I burst out crying. No one was moved by my emotion save the stallholder, who couldn't help but react at the sight of my tears.

Between sobs, I explained I was only visiting Yaoundé, and that if he wanted me to tend him, he'd have to come with me to my parents' house in Obala.

A slight graze swallowed everything that had been my life up until then, the serene image of which, when I had a quiet moment, continued to hover over the troubled waters of my new existence. I was fourteen years old.

▼

It all began with that moment of exuberance in front of the French apples, with a minor flesh wound that had resulted in the man demanding my hand in marriage. I had hoped to find refuge in Obala but my future husband insisted my father give his consent. A graze was all it took to cause everything to flow backwards; revolt itself perished in pockets of black water.

Even more portentous was the image of their discussion; men in jackets and old flannel trousers sitting cross-legged, deciding on my life, not allowing me to return to it. My eyes cast down, I would soon be leaving, like those individuals who had flitted through my childhood and continued to exist, to experience joys and sorrows far away and without my being there to see them.

I was wrenched from my family as I had always been wrenched from everything. I was still a child! I had been taken from my home in Obala and now my shattered dreams were urging me to return.

What fever had been goading me from the day I was born, the day I left my home, left my childhood and the guardian-spirits of the house? Everything had fallen apart the day my father gave into the black-mailer I'd injured with my parasol, and day by day it had continued to disintegrate.

I could still picture the scene: the amorphous shapes of hookah-smoking men, the flat reflections of shadows from behind, imagining the sign that showed weakening, consensus.

My life was about to change radically. I was going to have to leave my home and immediate family. The separation had begun. I cannot help returning to this, my broken destiny of woman, and reliving it with a sense of revolt.

Before setting off with my husband for Yaoundé and leaving Obala for ever, my mother's last words to me were, 'It is time for the chick to fly the nest. Before the next moon you will belong to the man who will use you as he will.'

My mother's verbal contortion reverberated in me. I had to accept the family ruling but it destroyed the sacred aura surrounding my love for my parents and put an end to my dreams of a different kind of life. I studied her from the inevitable distance that removes a chick from its nest.

4: My New Family

▼

Because of the dark maw that had suddenly opened when the door of the family home slammed behind me, because of the greyness of the bush-taxi that was taking my husband and me back to Yaoundé, the worthless ramparts that had for so long protected me crumbled the moment I raised my eyes to look at my husband.

He was a tall thin man. This impression was perhaps due to the slenderness of a face compatible with his height; the solemn, pensive, composed face of a man ready to tackle anything, that would express all kinds of changes. His features might herald anger closely followed by calm, then fear instantly followed by sorrow, while never completely revealing any of these. His was an utterly ambiguous, mysterious face; eyebrows raised in surprise, a direct gaze indicating honesty and decency; a flat turned-up nose that looked to be only flesh from bridge to tip, flared nostrils that suggested enthusiasm – or was it impetuosity? Lips as large as blocks of ebony, the full mouth of African carvings, of one who can see beyond appearances but betraying apathy too, an aptitude for nonchalance and infinite generosity; ears that strained to hear, although they would never hear the high-pitched cries of pain or maimed echoes of anguish and anxiety.

My husband's ears were too full of the mindless hubbub of Yaoundé: the screech of traffic, the din of bush-taxis, the whine of daytime activities and drone of commercial transactions. What helped me – not adapt to the wrench but, worn down with grief, not abandon myself completely to despair – was the thought of the young girls who, like me, had been taken from their families and given in marriage, as a result of being outsiders in the world.

In my head, I can still hear, and always will, the names of the many faces seen since childhood – Balbine, Pétronille, Domitilde – though I would remember them all if I saw them again, distorted by the film of memory.

I had difficulty recognising the woman who'd sold us doughnuts when I was a child; I imagined her life was a heavy burden on her shoulders, encumbering her movements, making her less self-assured, slower.

I can only just make out the features of the little girl – she never went to school either – sitting in the dust, rolling Hausa sweets on her thigh before selling them to passers-by.

The childish faces of the shyest of my village friends, those with whom I was never on intimate terms, are hazy now. I can still hear their names ring out as they did from the mouth of the village idiot as he taunted them: Crescence, Phénoména, Josephine. How sad to remember their names when I know I wouldn't be able to recognise them again!

Oh! The faces of the people who'd left us, the ones we couldn't hold on to, are gradually fading from our memory, these fleeting faces we see in mirages and musings.

Yes, that's why we were outsiders – because girls didn't go to school *because they were girls* – and that's why I developed a taste for revolt. I had carried the seed inside me since childhood and I rebelled hard against the segregation and strove or thought I strove to end it, but the damnation has not been broken. For a soul shaped by the sword that distorts it bears the scar for all time; and it's always the same struggle to scheme, the same attempt to escape as though from a siege, but as soon as the alarm sounds, it is the same rapid retreat, as my disintegrating life proved.

And should I now feel helpless for having found in my life with my husband, only *that* to challenge – my submissive childhood in Obala?

▼

During my first meal with my new family, I felt like a foreigner, uprooted. Emilia, my husband's first wife, laughed and talked to conceal her embarrassment, and encouraged me to eat. I felt that my childhood innocence was closing up behind me, that I had been driven out of Obala and thrown into another world that was somehow forbidden me: henceforth, I would remain suspended between the old universe, the only one that was real but to which I was barred from returning, and this new life that I felt compelled to challenge. On the one hand it was rejecting me – I could see that all too clearly from the scowls my husband's first two wives were giving me – and on the other hand, I was rejecting it. I never felt a part of the family; we were isolated, my son and I, rootless. Shame, bewilderment, the feeling that I was falling or being hounded into a corner – I experienced them all the moment I left Obala for Yaoundé.

The sense of discomfort, and soon of alienation, that I experienced during that very first meal with my new family, wasn't yet the feeling which came much later: that I was a skivvy.

My husband's wives would say, 'Tonight you will grind the millet, and then you will go down to the river to soak the washing. Tomorrow you will do the washing, and then you will join us in the fields. You are like the last weevil on earth who lays its eggs then dies; you are the last to arrive and you will obey us.'

When, the night of my arrival, I heard them give me orders, it seemed to me that something had begun to limp, that an unknown dissonance was wrecking the harmony of my life. I could have attributed the tone of the commands to language problems, and yet the idea never occurred to me. I never doubted for a moment that I was being given the most demeaning of tasks, and by the same token, I became convinced that real life was elsewhere, where I no longer was, that it would continue to be, and that it was the only livable life.

A shadow was beginning to invade the room I was in through the two low square windows that opened almost level with the ground. It would soon blow the fragile growth, so vulnerable, so fleeting, of the tall palmyra which, with its rounded fan-shaped leaves, provided the only shade in the courtyard.

It seemed to me that not a day went by when I didn't see from this opening, from the window of the communal room, my husband's isolated apartment that I so dreaded having to visit. I knew that once night had fallen, that once the dark outside had joined the dark inside, I would have to go to him and surrender myself to the horrors of entwining flesh.

▼

My fall took place, that very night, in a time preceding all memory.

For my rejection to have any significance, it had to be taken further – into wilderness and into fire – where I would be alone, where my soft face, with its gash of sensitive lips, would surrender to death, to the stern, withdrawn and incorruptible face of the thirty-three-year-old stranger who was my husband.

I had recognised in him, as in all men, the withdrawing, the restricting, the trampling of the soul, the contemptuous taciturnity that is the bed of the polygamist; and at the same time, a hunger for flesh and a predilection for the suffering and destruction of womanhood.

I felt, though I couldn't prove it, that for men feeling did not exist and that marriage, much like saliva, tears and blood, was an organic reality.

What could my young body, at the threshold of blood, have said about that night of aching womb and scattered pain, other than lose itself in a scream? In the harshness of embraces, I discovered the youthfulness of my flesh and sudden immodesty of my virginity, until I came apart from myself, left my soul and vanished like the sea retreating to its bed.

5: Amongst Women

▼

'Look at me, Ékéla. What are the seven commandments a wife must know?'

'I don't know, but you're going to teach me.'

'This is the exact wording.

One: know that a wife is created for a husband.
Two: never imagine there's any other man but your husband.
Three: love your husband.
Four: fear him.
Five: praise his name.
Six: show him obedience and gratitude or risk repudiation.
Seven: as the doe succumbs to the wolf so you must consent to be intimate with him.

'If you break just one of these commandments you will receive forty lashes less one.'

'But what if a stranger should turn up and force the woman to violate the law of fidelity, what does the law say about that?'

'It is better to die than to transgress. Tell me why the last to arrive does not have the same rights as the other wives.'

In the hazel eyes of Emilia, my husband's first wife, I saw a look of triumph that said, 'You will always be a slave, working yourself to death for your family, for the children who are not yours, sixteen hours a day – and don't you dare complain!'

'I'm waiting, Ékéla ...'

'Tradition ruled it would be so without consulting the last to arrive.'

'Have you forgotten who you're talking to! You owe me unconditional respect,' Emilia fumed. 'I am the first wife. Which means you owe me an explanation.'

'You are the beloved of our great, valiant, formidable, jealous and strong lord and master. He chose you first so that each year you might bear him another child.'

Emilia looked at me questioningly; ready to carve me out the worst fate she could.

'I think it's time we taught you your new duties,' said Anaba, who had remained hidden in the shadows, like a mango under a leaf. 'You are like the pangolin, the giant lizard whose eye glides over the swamp like a ball of ink predicting any change in the weather. You can't keep still; you are the impala who leaps about to escape the lioness but whose throat sooner or later is slit.'

From the disdain in her eyes I could see it would be dangerous to interrupt this first exchange between wives.

'You should know that here the man is the law,' Anaba continued. 'He will always come between you and your children. He will always take the little you have. You owe him everything and he owes you nothing. You are the clay vase waiting to be filled by him. You will remain empty and accessible to he who will never acknowledge you.'

Anaba's speech reverberated like the song of the swan. She was describing a life of abuse, and all I could do, in my threadbare *kaba*, was mutter, 'Yes,' and agree to everything.

'Why should you never raise your voice to your husband?' asked Emilia, who hadn't said a word for some time.

'Your shouts will wake no one.'

'Well done, Ékéla, you have proved just how perfidious you can be. You can now be admitted to the clan of women. The day will come when you will put your husband's future wives to the test.'

▼

It was with nostalgia that I would recall that first meeting with my husband's other wives, a nostalgia whose unpredictable emergence I dared not risk, for with the memory, the involuntary cruelty returned. Because the bond between me and the other wives was never stronger than during that test, images of shared experiences would flood back, threatening to reopen the deep-rooted hurt and revolt.

6: Recollections

▼

The fondest, most wounded of loves, even pain itself all have their dark night. The wilderness, the grief – why did they have to enter my new life, almost like a rebirth? Why did I have to experience them then?

I had never known such blissful happiness when I lived with my parents, and that dismal day with its unremitting rain and flurries of dust served only to intensify it. Such pain, could it be that it has the same mask or face as the harsh tradition that demands that blue alleviate our grief? My anger, though I endeavoured to conceal it, could so easily have exploded at the slightest provocation.

I see my child Douo again. At night, he loved me to stay with him until he fell asleep; to sing, not songs, for I didn't know any, but the melodies I used to sing in the Marist church in Obala. Night after night I had to sing him his favourite one. How old would he have been then – three maybe? He never grew tired of it. Does he remember it wherever he is now? It was 'As a deer longs for flowing streams, so my soul longs for You, O God.' Or St Francis of Assisi's prayer: 'Lord, make me an instrument of Your peace. Where there is hatred, let me sow love. Where there is injury, pardon. Where there is doubt, faith. Where there is darkness, light ...'

I had always given my dresses names. There was my bluish-green juice-of-cassava-leaf dress and my viper-black dress. Floating tunics, flower-shaped bubus, loincloths I tied over my stomach. Viper! Or an even deeper black – palm-oil black. He loved that name, it made him laugh; it was a shade of black that soap couldn't touch. The names described the banality of colours so Douo invented more poetic names.

My rainy season *kaba* dress was the 'bird of paradise'. A swarm, a swirl of blue clouds with, at their heart, barely visible golden alluvia. I wore it the day we went to the Central Market, when chatting together, we took the narrow hibiscus-lined track home. Does he remember the long stop we made on the wooden bridge where we watched the Ewoé, the River of Smiles, flowing below us? What could we have been thinking about, the two of us there, not saying a word?

Ah, the memories we both had, connected to each dress, memories that were always evoked by them, that appeared in his eyes as he stood in the doorway. I was wearing the dress he named 'bird of paradise'; I was wearing it one afternoon in the rainy season, a weekday. My husband wasn't with us. He'd gone to play *songo*, or draughts, and anyway, he wouldn't have been interested; he'd have just shrugged his shoulders. So we'd gone, just the two of us on our own to look at the bamboos and giant frogs Douo called 'leapfrogs'.

These private holidays of ours we repeated, my son and I. The memory of them took root and glowed in him, in me. This fond memory, the words he sometimes spoke, his awareness: nothing was without significance.

Today there is an insurmountable distance between us, and I can find no crack, no gap in this act of violence that has exiled us from each other. My grief has been secretly nurtured by my love for the child I have lost; today I have become the grief into which I have retreated, and all I have left from my first son is the icy calm that lives on in the humming-bird blue of my *kaba* or palm-flower blue of my loin-cloth while love is no longer there to give light.

One day, you find all you have left are memories to be shelled, mixed and spread like groundnuts in the courtyard. And as you strip them of their brownish skin, you realise you have nothing, that perhaps you never had anything; and it is always the same memories that lead you further still, to all the places you once passed through, where for a split second you lived and breathed. Those dazzling minutes, already disappeared on the horizon, still shine like the look in Douo's eyes before he was snatched from me. Everything else had already been submerged and by the time I had captured this final light, I was swallowed up with him for ever.

These images, what power they have over me! Some blind me, like that of my first encounter with my husband, crystallised in my fifteenth year, but gradually transformed – that look, increasingly more absent, more empty, when, to protect myself from the last rays of the setting sun, I struck him in the face with my parasol.

That vivid, painful image I had taken away with me is what I saw before falling asleep, pacified.

I always feel the same fascination, the same insatiable need to dwell on the clumsy, unconscious act that determined my destiny. There are memories I shall continue to examine all my life without ever being able to understand them, so insignificant do they appear to be. Hence the long monologue, the angry words, the curses he hurled at me that terrified me so – those unforgettable words that sealed my fate, what is left of them now? The heated words have fled and ended up stranded in indifference.

And so my regret at not refusing his demand to minister to him grew ever deeper. And with it came flooding back a thousand half-forgotten details that loomed larger than life. It was as though I were being reproached for not having paid them enough attention. Would I never be able to put the past behind me? And where would I find my second wind, I who had lived so little and so unsatisfactorily?

So sad were some of these memories, some of these sensations, that I was forced to tear myself away from them so as not to become embittered. All I had to do was shut my eyes and I was back in the past looking at the objects I tremble to describe.

Back in the half-light of the communal room I bumped into the rocking chair, buried my pain in the rattan bed, beat the floor with my fists, the dust-covered floor I couldn't see though it bore me, where memory had dug holes I stubbornly refused to acknowledge.

Stumbling on past joys, as on a pebble in the grass, I felt I was being returned to my lost child.

I'm in my room; the doors are the depth and absence of colour. Douo is there waiting for me. He has black eyes, not brown like most Africans, a pitch-black, palm-oil black, blue-black I've never seen in anyone else; bewitching, at times sombre, at others lively, prone to few variations. The child is there, his eyes, his face in front of me. I touch him, I breathe him, I hold him to me.

Had I not experienced this happiness, this bliss, at least once with Douo, and not in the wilderness of dreams, but in the reality of the world? The steadfast light was, I knew, the flame of maternal love, for five years, from my fifteenth to my twentieth year, harmony, a whispered joy that nothing could corrupt.

The memory of it is mine, and it is permeated with the same soft gentle rocking movements.

7: Shame

▼

The shame of being a woman started when I was still a child, for the pride it gave me was badly shaken when I heard men declare I was good for nothing except having babies.

We have to understand that our sensitivity, our tears, our screams of pain in labour embarrass men, just as the immense split of womanhood offends them. Our animal-like whimpers, our moans at dawn, life's difficulties that wear us down, are like the hum of insects, the polecat of resentment sniffing out death among the giant coconut palms. The same wail that rises from the depths is hurled at the sky's empty face.

My life was empty of joy, empty of pleasure. Because they were stronger than me, I couldn't rid myself of the guilt and anguish that tormented me.

Douo's expression, his face, would so often appear with almost unbearable clarity that I experienced all over again the bitter regret I had felt the day he was abducted.

I would have liked to say no to life because it had eluded me since childhood. I was lost and abandoned; only dreams could allay my fears. I had no interest in anything. Weak with despair, awake at night and during the long hours of daybreak, I felt that the future held nothing but disintegration. It crossed my mind that I should bury myself in Yaoundé, alone and far from anyone, even my family.

The hours I spent deliberating the matter nearly drove me crazy. I was getting used to his absence. I was taming the hurt. The shard still flayed the past I dreamed of hiding in. I had never felt safe in the bosom of the new family into which I had been brought, to share the secrets of a world far larger than that of my early childhood. At barely twenty I, Sabeth, felt a dark thrill grip my heart at the thought that my life didn't belonged to me and that it was I who had acquiesced to this.

I spent a lot of time in the kitchen, walking around it slowly, starting at the mud wall to the left of the door as you go in. In the middle, opposite the window, there's a rectangular mahogany table, and on either side, small benches and a rattan chair. I was attracted to the wicker baskets hanging on the wall high above the table. Was it the thought of the smoked meat, the supplies of sorghum and millet that protected us – my husband, the other wives and me – from famine?

On the ground I found the aluminium pots Hausas made by melting down old tin cans. I was happy; I'd boil some milk, add cane sugar and stir it into sorghum flour mixed with a little water. Pouring the boiling milk, I'd watch the skin wrinkle slightly, and with a wooden spoon I'd stir the sorghum to stop it from sticking. I'd let it simmer for four or five minutes before adding butter and a handful of fresh ginger. Ginger brings out the flavour, the spices and the exquisite aroma of the sorghum cream, and celebrates the exhilaration of desire – the never-ending wound which is an essential part of the reality of polygamy.

And I went to love as I went to sin. That evening, I knew I'd have to go to my husband, the owner who wanted to be sole ruler of all women, who felt dispossessed at the slightest lapse. And is the opaque stone inside him the dark glow that comes from lack of love?

One night, because I wouldn't open my mouth to his tongue which, like a prey, like a hunted lizard, wanted to force its way in; moaning, thrashing his head from side to side, the man flogged me.

Where did my revulsion – as though I were being attacked by an unknown animal – suddenly come from? Why, on that particular night, did I feel reduced to a body, no, not even a body, a function? One of the other wives could have done just as well.

So why the agony, why the shame when I passed the other women as I crossed the courtyard? Through one of the skylights in the raffia roof of my husband's small house, he was watching the sun set on the mountain opposite; its peak would soon turn crimson. This momentary malaise caused the sensitive parts of my body to tense up, and the colours of the world suddenly became exaggerated and unfamiliar, harsh and disquieting like a groan.

Whence came my detachment, my revolt which, with every night that passed, served to reinforce my anger, to anchor it more firmly, more fiercely?

I retreated further into silence. What could I have said, how could I have stood up for myself, and what would have been the point? Why could I – who up until then, like a planet craving light, had given myself and looked to this man for everything – no longer bear my husband's hostile body on me?

It wasn't me my husband possessed, but my rejection which tensed, which stiffened in entwinings that no satiety could disentangle; and there was that other part of me that eluded him, that escaped him, and that he would perhaps never be able to reach.

8: In the Fields

▼

Once Douo had gone, the only thing that could tear me from the clamminess of my straw bed was the first song of the partridge. I made my way to the fields.

Every time I woke it was to find the same sharp, unbearable thorn inside me, aggravated by years of self-sacrifice and a growing recognition of my degradation. Crushed by the shock, I found myself unable to merge with this life of freedom, to forget or lose myself.

The village was still sleeping. With my basket on my back and a machete in my hand so I could clear a path through the fields of briars I'd chant as I trampled the dew that exploded underfoot into resonant droplets.

To live demanded a superhuman effort that left me spent.

The birdsong in the woods, the air curling around the flowers as they unfolded, the toads trembling in the marshland shade made me feel that the dance of death was about to begin and that my body would soon be passing on.

In much the same way that we learn to breathe, so I tamed the earth; I contemplated each stab of the rain, in much the same way that we discover faces.

From far away, daylight seeped through to me. The savannah was enveloped in a humid mellowness that removed it from reality. The sultriness hazed the gnarled trunks of the forest.

Halfway up the frangipani trees I could see a pale orangey-rimmed shadow; each branch was laced with light and over there, taciturn and mysterious, a kingdom kept vigil, rooted in patience.

I concentrated all my efforts on the immediate landscape – euphorbia and pandanaceae, their trunks smoothed with blackened silver, sun-splashed potholes, warm white light – that urged me to quicken my step. It was the middle of the dry season I so dreaded; it was always an ordeal.

We had believed in the blossoming of days and life was filling with stars, emptied of signs. The drought was devouring the landscape as time came to a standstill.

Dawn was so beautiful it hurt; a smooth sparkling birth that gave depth to the world, presented the whole universe and with it the memory of the child loved too much and lost.

The abduction was continually reborn in my memory.

The child, I worshipped him in every drop of our lakes and rivers, in the flow of the River Wouri, in the splendour of the hibiscus and the bite of the wind. Wherever I looked I saw him – in the countless constellations and the most secluded corner of the forest, in the mounds of turned earth and the mists flushed by sunrise, in the grassland plateau and the sands born in the aftermath of the deluge.

As far back as I could remember, this was the moment of the day when I felt most at one with the world. Transmitting its vibrations to the sky, the light glistened a shimmering black, and it felt as though the forest, draining its branches one by one, was transforming the glow into the brightness of day.

More confident, I continued on my way, filled with the painful acceptance of what was to come. I needed to feel at the heart of the world, to brush against the still damp lower branches, to have my nostrils inhale the heady fragrance of the sap-filled leaves.

The darkness hung from wine palms that captured the light in diaphanous clouds, allowing the eye to glimpse only the density of the foliage that fell to the ground with funereal majesty.

The heaviness of the baobab trees was oppressive; it foretold a taking root, a vegetal burying.

The heat brought out the scent of the barks, lichens and resins. I moved through the elusive breath of an unexplored universe, penetrated the dense, the palpable sweltering heat.

The candelabra-euphorbia raised high their foliage. They stood aloof; their milky sap turned black by the air had congealed into a glutinous substance so dark it suddenly made the sky look pale. The branches drew the humidity which, combined with the smell of resin, thickened; as I reached out my hand, the stale acrid smell came to me.

This sign of communion, this participation in the world reassured me.

This dreamlike drifting went on for a long time. It was the screech of the owl that roused me from my reverie. I didn't like the mournful hooting, the bane of the sleeper, that rent a hole in the darkness.

I shuddered. It had seemed to me that the nocturnal bird of prey had cursed me and that I was unable to protect myself. I shut my eyes and imagined I could hear the forest grow. The world was bewitched and reverberated at last in its innermost depths.

9: The Blue of an African Morning

▼

Every time I think of the tradition that involves making a gift of your child to God or to those you love I feel a sense of revolt. To me, loss and rebellion are inextricably linked.

There were times when only the grunting of the warthog quelled my anger. I didn't like its doleful belligerent cry that rent the mist.

During the rainy season, the astringent moistness of mosses helped liberate the forest's secret ripening. The vegetation fed on the wonderful decomposition created by the humidity. It needed this deadly combination so that it could infuse me and thereby return me to the world.

The unbearable mugginess would drive me to a clearing or the edge of the wood. After the oppressiveness of the shade, the brilliance of the dandelions brought instant relief. The reprieve relaxed me and seeing the sky again, I was able to surrender myself to the forest. The astonishing and nourishing taste of the first guavas and taros I would forever associate with the forest.

Today, the glade is still airy, having been cleared of brambles and creepers. The prickly rustlings of the living undergrowth, the leaves scattered by the wind, the saplings – all contrasted sharply with the trunks sticky with humidity whose blackness and graininess rekindled my childhood aversion for certain mangrove trees whose fruit seemed to emerge from the rich soil by themselves.

Under cover, the near stifling heat spilled out. My

leaden feet kept sinking into the spongy carpet of dead leaves. My nostrils tingled with the smell of fresh mushrooms and acacia. I kept inhaling the delightful and elusive scent of earth, which then pulsed mysteriously before slipping away.

I was taming the subtle blue of African mornings. Times long-gone appeared in the landscape. The sky lit up and wove golden threads into the swathes of euphorbia. The air wore a different countenance. And it was against this hazy backdrop, like a misty blink, that reality, having finally consented to show itself, approached.

The thin light made the fragrant palm trees quiver. Would everything be taken from me before I grew old, I who was no longer attached to anything apart from the child I'd already lost and whose absence I would eventually have to accept?

I'd have done better to stick to the narrow track with the horizon hidden from view, to make my solitary way to the nascent light through the dust of days whose remnants were like a summons; and to avoid stumbling upon any semblance of harmony, through an unexpected encounter with sleeping waters, until after many a detour. Perhaps I needed to get right away from things?

The screw pine thinned out, and here and there, tree stumps broke through the surface of dead leaves. As I walked, the heady scent of absent flowers was like a challenge to memory. At last I spied a field swathed in the light of a season whose early morning fluctuations can be quite stunning. In an unstoppable movement the baobab reared above the mist to attack the sky.

Trampling the mud where the forest spirits lived, I was the wood set alight and left to go out. Now that my child was gone I would be easier to light than resin wood.

As sure as sludge and silt are pervious to light, so I would be reborn in the morning. It was good to be in the forest. It was the only thing to sparkle, adorned as it was with ribbons of numb dripping darkness. Through the red dust of the harmattan, I watched flickering reflections form faintly coloured rings around the trunks of trees – different degrees of grey that the eye could perceive though it was quite unable to describe the subtlety of their hues. I felt both surprise and elation at the sight of nature in all her glory.

Patches of dried-up grass and shrivelled shrubs had been caught unawares by the rain, and I saw the benumbed hawthorn and horsetail raise their ghostly shadows. The population of euphorbia seemed to have moved away. God's silence had gouged the smooth stems of the cotton plants whose leaden grey was unsettling. The flora had become rare. Here and there, tree stumps, like glossy black islets, had broken through the waterlogged surface of leaves – vibrating in their hidden depths, their colours were breathtaking. The tansy dripped, adjusting to the water from the sky that abandoned its vagaries to become long nourishing draughts to make sap flow.

The whole of nature was living in the rain's breath. From close up I could see the heavy drops, as one by one they broke loose. They were irresistibly mesmerising. I grabbed the sodden end of a branch and shook it; rain cascaded down and refreshed me from top to toe. In a fragile silence the whole forest dripped dry. The dank odour filled me with glee; it smelled of tansy, of earth-washed bark, with the occasional peppery waft or musky breeze from the hills of Yaoundé.

10: To Be Like Ékéla

▼

The K that cuts through my name, meaning goat, will sever my soul. Ékéla is the name given me the day I was born. My identity beaten out of me, my womanhood took refuge in the sacrificial goat, the one tradition named Ékéla. Woman and goat joined in the cruelty of ritual sacrifice. A knife between his teeth, humiliation opened my birth on to the vertigo of the wound of my sex.

I am the ruminant that ingests the sins of the world, the victim offered up to the sun, for whom to breathe is already an impossible act, and who, reaching the peak of herself, is toppled by the first breeze to come along.

Was my behaviour, the way I moved, not affected right from the start by this name, Ékéla? When I consider the thousand little details that shaped my goat-destiny, there are times when I tell myself that their very insignificance is worth saving since these elusive trifles – the rope slipped around Ékéla's neck that only she can break, the capricious leaps for which she was renowned, her irritating bleat that made her the perfect sacrificial victim – these fleeting images which have in fact not fled, are persistently reborn to bring me the same great joy or the same hidden pain.

It might have been better if I'd been a shepherdess or a goat. I could at least have run away rather than stand by and witness my own humiliation. I shall probably never scale great heights, never cross the desert, never suffer hunger. I shall probably never reach the level of indifference that leaves the goat skinned, offered up to the sun of a destructive madness. I shall probably never be constantly masticating like her, presenting the eternal return, an end to the resentment of time.

The wisdom of the goat is that she knows that everything comes round, accepts it and wouldn't want it any other way. She lives for the moment, producing lush foliage in the shade of which she is lively and capricious, revelling in the wild irrational joy of forgetting herself.

Imbued with the sign of strangeness, the rebellious goat conjures a magical past. From her spine to her horns, images subtly unfurl on the slenderness of her back. The river of memories, an individual's inner life that wells up and flows free and comes together to form only one, always the same, the call each time of the same journey, the sibylline frontier between life and death.

The world comes to me – smooth, opaque, unexpected, feral and gentle as though it had suddenly been tamed.

There alone had the end of resentment burned, where annihilation and annihilated came together as one. There is no other world to which I can return but to that shore of images – mortal and saved like the world that will be no more until the goat draws her last breath – images with which I shall sleep for ever, in which I shall bury myself.

Now that I had lost Douo I couldn't stand my goat-name that suggested I was in the dark, that I was marking time, fumbling around in a world open to another dimension that first haunted me then retreated. Revolt erupted. I was obsessed by the idea of breaking loose, of being reborn.

When I was young I dreamed of, or should I say envisioned, down to the last detail, living a life of anonymity delighting in the sacred. A focused, persistent, liberating dream. All the same it struck me as strange that I couldn't stop thinking about my childhood ambitions, recalling them more with hope than with shame.

I had forgotten nothing of all that. On the contrary, my visions served to ferment my future and my wish to be baptised. Other people probably have crazy ideas too, only their ideas don't stay with them for so long. They don't keep cropping up throughout their lives, beckoning to them in that familiar way, not sure they will be as well received by them as by me.

Moreover, without my having noticed the warning signs, the wheel had begun to turn. At the age of twenty, after Douo was abducted, had I not agreed to be a catechumen, to look after the sacristy whenever Father Delanoé asked me to? Not that there was anything religious about the room; it looked ordinary enough, with its few bits of functional furniture, and there was nothing in this sacristy of mine that scared me either.

For me it was a pleasurable sensation each time I thought of the host Father Delanoé gave out every Sunday in the chapel of Charles-Luanga in Yaoundé. I wasn't too sure what a host was, except that it was the Eucharist, but due to our ignorance of such things, due to their being beyond our understanding and consequently more alluring, my imagination was held spellbound by that clear syllable *host* and had turned it into a fundamental hieratic delicacy – a sliver of wheaten bread, often unleavened, forbidden, and therefore succulent – because on it depended the doctrine of transubstantiation that I hoped one day to taste.

And although the consecrated host – in the ciborium beneath the finely wrought gold frame of the tabernacle, the small alabaster columns, the mahogany body supported by a red pedestal – retained nothing of the god it incarnated, but was there to sublimate Him in every respect, I, the sexton, would spend hours on end staring at the hole, my gestures, my barely formulated thoughts, sometimes sanctifying sometimes pathetic, in a morning-long trance during which time I became one with the Eucharistic. And that is what drove me, despite the fear of punishment, despite the remorse, to steal the body of Christ and conceal it close to my heart.

I really thought I was some kind of monster. I was horrified at myself. I thought I'd never be reconciled either with myself or with God. Today the smell of toast still goes right through me and my heart skips a beat. I probably believe I still haven't been forgiven.

I was both sad and thrilled at having been deprived of the sacred since birth. There was already a sense of dereliction – as the wife of a polygamist I was prohibited from taking the sacraments – and I was convinced that once I was dead, I would be no more than a pile of dust that would soon be hidden from the eyes of men.

It was the wish to be saved that I'd had since childhood, and which had grown out of my great respect for the Holy Book, not to mention some mysterious fetishism or other, that prompted me to carry out my theft.

For like all black women I had always frequented witchdoctors and knew that muddled superstition and divinity meant I would find it hard not to give in to panic when night fell.

▼

However fervent my aspirations, they weren't strong enough to help me overcome my fears and I hadn't been able to bring myself to swallow the stolen host I kept close to my heart.

I tried to calm my palpitations, which fear alone had not provoked, reminding myself of the protective power of blood offered as a libation during sacrificial rituals.

I dared not take the host out of my pocket for fear of stripping it of its protective power but I would touch it all the time and hold it in my clammy fingers.

These crazy notions, through the additional freedom they had given me, drew me away from the physical pain of working the land. The protracted inactivity I indulged in, in the sacristy, only served to deepen my unhappiness and euphoria at being thus deprived of everything. Already I could feel, deep inside me, a sense of bitterness growing out of my mysterious aspiration to liberty.

11: My Baptismal Name

▼

I, Ékéla, would never have thought of opening the evangelistary. I couldn't even read. However, during the months that followed my catechumenate, I found myself having to tackle another problem, difficult to put into words, and one with which no one could help me.

In truth I was fretting over the name given me by my tribe. I was troubled by the profane meaning with which it was saddled. What should be my baptismal name?

Every time I had to utter my name, Ékéla, my tongue would go all over the place. I knew the name had the power to take over and control the soul. My mind was beset by strange deliberations, in which a saint's particular protective power was combined with the magical belief in the nature of things.

In his catechism class, Father Delanoé said that baptism imposed a name on the soul and that that name decided what the soul should become. Therefore to know the meaning and purpose of the name allowed the bearer of the name to know what would become of him in this life and the next.

One day, during the Mass for the first Sunday of Advent, Father Delanoé read the first chapter of the Gospel according to St Luke:

> 'In the days when Herod was King of Judea, there was a priest called Zachary, of Abia's turn of office, who had married a wife of Aaron's family, by name Elizabeth; they were both well

approved in God's sight, following all the commandments and observances of the Lord without reproach. They had no child; Elizabeth was barren, and both were now well advanced in years. He, then, as it happened, was doing a priest's duty before God in the order of his turn of office; and had been chosen by lot, as was the custom among the priests, to go into the sanctuary of the Lord and burn incense there, while the whole multitude of the people stood praying without, at the hour of sacrifice. Suddenly he saw an angel of the Lord, standing at the right of the altar where incense was burnt. Zachary was bewildered at the sight, and overcome with fear; but the angel said, "Zachary, do not be afraid; thy prayer has been heard, and thy wife Elizabeth is to bear thee a son, to whom thou shalt give the name of John. Joy and gladness shall be thine, and many hearts shall rejoice over the birth, for he is to be high in the Lord's favour; he is to drink neither wine nor strong drink; and from the time when he is yet a child in his mother's womb he shall be filled with the Holy Ghost. He shall bring back many of the sons of Israel to the Lord their God, ushering in his advent in the spirit and power of Elias. *He shall unite the hearts of all, the fathers with the children.*"'

▼

To take the name of Elizabeth would be to offer my soul the possibility of a singular destiny, the hope that one day my son *would unite the hearts of all, the fathers with the children.*

Until I was brought to the baptismal font, until Father Delanoé put salt on my lips, anointed my brow with holy chrism and gave me the name I had chosen, I was blinded by tears. Was I still the sacrificed goat, drained and dried like an angel of salt, or was I now another, waking up in the beneficent, living presence of a beatified person, that of Elizabeth? Is that what baptism was, a rupture, a sudden distancing from tradition, like an icy game with identity?

And yet, I had never felt so close to myself, no, never. Liberated by pain and brought closer to the sacred by Saint Elizabeth, I had never felt so close to happiness as on the day I was baptised when, having been inducted into the mysterious reality of the soul, I felt that, like Zachariah's wife, the Angel Gabriel had visited me.

12: I Meet Ma

▼

At first, surprise – is that all baptism was? Father Delanoé wore, as he did for High Mass, one of those immaculate chasubles with only a narrow purple stole around his neck to set him apart from the secular and emphasise the magnificent distance that brought him closer to God.

The choirboy led the way. Both he and the Father walked with the same solemn gait. The tinkling of the bell in the boy's hand soared like a flock of starlings.

Surely that couldn't be the baptismal font, an ordinary basin covered with banana leaves, which the choirboy – eyes down, candle in hand – was approaching? The light rose straight and bright to the chapel roof and beyond, higher and higher still, to the sun that a flock of starlings was devouring – visible image of God's inaccessible, unimaginable and sublime truth.

What I, Ékéla, expected, promised by and contained in the Roman syllables of Elizabeth; what I watched for in the distance, was a pomp more beautiful and more moving than on the eve of the Nativity, when the Divine Child in a moment of intense silence finally takes His place in the crib; it was the solemnity of the processions that greeted the Archbishop, on one of his rare visits, in the square of the Cathedral of Notre-Dame of Yaoundé, the visible manifestation of the sacred, the blaze of crimson and gold.

At first, surprise – there was only Father Delanoé, so unremarkable, so poor an orator, the disappointment in the sigh that greeted his stepping into the pulpit on Sundays.

I repeated the words – *this is my baptism* – examined them as I would a guava, opened them, rummaged around inside them, going deeper and deeper in search of memory's juice.

Destroyed, nullified, the ordinary yet extraordinary presence of Father Delanoë standing next to the baptismal font, I stared at the stained-glass window in front of me; with each step I took it grew larger. It was all I could see, the image of Elizabeth on the day the Virgin Mary visited her following the Annunciation, and the two children trembling in their mothers' wombs.

The pale glow of the stained-glass window disappeared inside me as if swept away by the muffled tinkling of the bell, and as Father Delanoë and the choirboy gradually drew near, a different ache welled up and supplanted the holy image.

As Father Delanoë bade the godmother come forward, incense misted the candlelight, and I again experienced a feeling of ecstasy, a sudden fragile encounter, a magical and overpowering fusing of an old emotion with the birth of a new identity.

All at once I thought I was near enough to touch the veiled dark waters of my godmother's eyes; I thought I heard her breath, her hushed but clear song. It was as though Mamie Titi had just opened the door of my memory, as though her words as they fell were weaving the thread of a new fabric around me.

I can still picture my meeting with Mamie Titi – all those African women destined, through their work in the fields, to be the guardians of time that they enfold in their enormous flavour- and perfumed-filled flesh. Mamie Titi's warm strength led women into physical depths where they could rest and dream. Crouched, feet apart under their loincloths, they'd sway gently and softly sing ancestral songs that maybe the roots of the rosewood could hear.

Mamie Titi honoured the forest filled with occult forces and stirred the songs of the breeze and the bowels of the earth. The landscape, broken up into meadows and groves, was a constant delight that we praised with more passion than the great church festivals.

The sweltering heat of tropical thickets gave way to the invigoration of intoxication; when freed from care we'd sing quietly and gracefully. The chanting would go on for hours; it rose up, bursting in the youth of our breasts and the vigour of our limbs. I discovered I had always lived in a state of alertness, driven from within by a tension so great that it propelled me into ritual acts and hasty reactions to events.

Living a life of compliance, as I strove to find a way round my husband's wishes, had eroded my painstakingly acquired identity.

In the fields, eyes blinded by the light, head spinning from the relentless motion of the hoe, even as I sang or chanted rather than sang, I was giving in to indolence, becoming resigned to the world.

And the world had Mamie Titi's face and body. I was mesmerised by the face advancing towards me, black like the face of the first woman I ever saw, like the face of the first woman. So steadfast was the apparition that I began to wonder whether this woman, who was said to have the gift of healing, was my guardian angel or the shadow of my angel?

I smiled and Mamie Titi smiled back, revealing the beauty of her teeth. In that extraordinary moment, I observed a mouth, perfectly delineated, and the sensuality of lips part closed over their secrets, part open over teeth still white despite her age. I was suddenly conscious of my own lips, the irregularity of my breaths drawn out of my body and expelled by my voice. I saw too how Mamie Titi's posture exuded a natural elegance, and how moved she was by the pure joy of sharing that was urging me in her direction. Her gestures reflected an air of absolute nobility and patient humility.

The old lady was with me the day I was brought to the baptismal font. Father Delanoé put salt on my lips, anointed my brow with holy chrism and water and gave me the Christian name of Elizabeth, in the name of the Father and of the Son and of the Holy Ghost.

Mamie Titi, who had not been baptised, spoke the name heavy with religious significance. The name would bring with it humility and obedience to the divinity, as was the case with Zachariah's wife who late in life had carried the first of the baptisers. By choosing the name of Elizabeth I was offering myself an opportunity I'd never had.

The moment the ceremony was over Father Delanoé withdrew to the sacristy. Mamie Titi touched me on the shoulder and said, 'I shall call you Sabeth, for we take a name to take root in another's heart and to live like a parasite in a memory that isn't ours.'

In that extraordinary moment of my rebirth, I felt my lips part, draw level then touch those of Mamie Titi. I murmured, Ma, protracting the cry my child had uttered. The word filled my mouth with pleasure.

Never forget the hour of mystery, never forget the healer's song, for the world will never rise from the waters until woman inhabits the heavens, until woman regulates the course of the stars and the gods, until in her resounds the sound – Ma – the syllable that governs the melodies time forgot.

In all its manifestations I see it – in the beautiful water where the watercress quivers, in the silky carp, in clay, in mud, in the rose so glorious in its mirror where, uninterrupted, its path and its passing are renewed – Ma, magical syllable that breathes life into matter, footsteps of lost days, visibility of breath and ferment of the mind.

13: Rebellion

▼

Strange pain, on hearing of my father's death. Fear, childhood memories came flooding back, leaving me gasping for air and, with each day that passed, more sensitive than before.

My father, dead! Did that mean, and was that what I wanted, that every bit of the invisible fabric that was wrapped around me was gone? By leaving Obala, then by being baptised, I thought I had changed worlds as absolutely as Elias who, in a flaming chariot, went up on a whirlwind to heaven.

I, this woman tormented by childhood, with a husband, a family, who had started on the downward slope of her life – what a struggle it was not to sink completely, now that our father had left us!

However hard I tried it was a female sensitivity I could no longer ignore, having survived the death or loss of people I loved, having survived the disappearance of all the actions, the deeds that had combined to weigh me down or become rooted deep within me.

Was it possible that it had taken only six years to forge this sensitivity? Did I know that with the images of the first funeral – the sacrificial goat that purifies the sons of the tribe, the incense, the foundation stone reminiscent of a huge navel, the mourners' voices at the graveside – others would appear? Did I know myself – so often in the world of tears – having been, before my revolt, so brutally wrenched from myself? All those women's faces with their auras so bright that I feared my mother might be accused of my father's death.

I suppose I had always somehow known it was mythology that had cast woman as the evil character, and my rebellion had only served to drive home the myth and its many strange associations.

The village wise men had a story that told how woman had been the bringer of death. As it was her responsibility to feed the family, she'd go into the forest every day where she was plagued by demons who'd whisper threats in her ears and raise flames near her face and claws to tear at her flesh. The village men had warned her that death was roaming the forest and that they were in great peril. On her way to the forest one day the woman came upon a lizard. While she was wondering how she could get the huge lizard back to the village, it spoke to her. 'And what if I were to take *you* back to *my* village?'

Fear, anger, temptations of all kinds flashed through her mind. The woman exclaimed, 'Goodness, lizard, what if you were this death that the villagers have been talking about?' To protect herself from death's malign influence, the woman ran to the edge of the marshlands and washed her hands, pretending that nothing had happened.

But the lizard wasn't going to give up that easily. 'Woe betide you if you leave me here and woe betide you if you take me with you.' Petrified, the woman tried again to protect herself and she said, 'So be it, but how am I to get you into the village?'

'Bend down and let me enter where men come into the world.'

Thus secreted in the darkness of the woman's womb, death entered the village.

My father's death unlocked something inside me and although I was more broken than before, somehow I felt liberated from the paternal yoke. But the burden of my mother's guilt, her need to atone, to take full responsibility for his death only added to my distress.

Was it the lure of madness or of renunciation? In Africa renunciation has the face of woman, of she who made men mortal by carrying the lizard in her womb. But how can it have the face of woman? And the renunciation of what? Of happiness? Of womanhood? After all, women only aspire to reawaken happiness and it was a cry of hope that at this moment escaped my distraught mother's lips.

How many more times would it return, the absurd and monotonous supplication that poured out of me each day? May the journey I have been given to undertake last right to the end, right up to my death, though nothing will remain of it save a glimmer of hope. Though the only thing to distinguish it from death will be the glimmer, the irregular breathing, the thumping heart that will survive all else. It is still not quite a farewell, not the outrageous, incomprehensible absence.

A funeral is also a refusal, an inability to forget. It prevents the wound from ever healing; it keeps the wound open to the lightness of life, plunges back into it and deepens itself.

When confronted with death, what still matters? Revolt maybe, the starkness of a cry or a farewell, the sudden tremor, the searing of the heart.

Revenge, punishment, hexes; I have always despised a tradition that lays the blame on woman. Was this only just sinking into me, like a vague but dangerous ferment that would rise later? Whence came my revolt at the recollection of the pond's milky bed, the trace, suspended above a spongy meadow studded with clumps of rushes, halfway between heaven and earth? Thinking about it again, I would have liked to enter my mother's skin, to bathe with her in the waters of desolation, to become one with her.

Had I ever really believed in the ceremony that identifies the guilty party, or that everything was already written, and that all that was required was a signature, for whatever tradition had determined, to become reality?

At that moment in time, it was against the tyranny of another injunction that I was rebelling, the one that had taken my first child from me.

I didn't even know what it was I was challenging – possibly revolt at the thought of what my mother was going through. I can still see her there in the pond waiting for the wicker basket left by one of the elders to float her way. I knew what my mother was experiencing; I knew what it was to feel lost and to have no hope of finding myself again.

I haven't finished remembering. A whole new life would not be time enough to relive my mother's shame, the degradation to which I saw her sink, submerged in water, a willing victim waiting for the basket to identify her as the guilty party. For someone must be guilty of every man's death. And the law of nature demands the basket drift towards anyone who disturbs its calm waters.

Man is the one who remembers and who is remembered. Woman has no need to be remembered. She is like the basket through which water passes, the goatskin dimpled by man's thirst.

Whilst I was moved by my mother's humiliation and felt closer to her, by the sorry spectacle of a life doomed from the start, by the proclamation of her guilt, by the renunciation of the world of the living that had, in and by and through sorrow, revealed the constraints of our condition, I could not forgive her for having allowed herself to sink so low.

Yes, hate welled up more often, and like a fig on thistles I found it more difficult to suppress it. It was the shard of resentment stabbing me.

I will always feel this weight, and this revolt whenever I remember the basket that stopped in the middle of the pond, refusing to find my mother guilty.

All eyes had been on her, emotion suspended, the sudden accusation, like an icy game with grief – and yet never had I felt so close to her, no, never. Spurred on by my own misery, brought closer to death by her, never before had I felt I was in her, that I moved with her shivering body beneath the pale moon, *that I was her*.

14: Requiem

▼

Anguish rises, spreads and envelops me like a tide come from below the horizon that had never before reached so far up the banks of the River Foulou. No retreat, no pebble is left untouched; it engulfs everything it touches, like this lifeless, dying love, drained of everything save the fear that refuses to acknowledge and accept my father's death. Trembling and shouting, my fear left me inconsolably grateful to memory.

Memory's sharp edge shines, as though a new wave of light were flowing over and covering the old, obliterating and transforming it. I shut my eyes. I open my eyes. The bamboo bed is there, the corpse limp and dazed, covered over with a blue sheet, henceforth immobile. It is your image, Father, that I find there, that I embrace. You are all I see there, stretched out, offered, familiar; everything is familiar – the corpse, the village of my childhood, Obala, the declining afternoon. The village's tiny heart has stopped separating nothing, from childhood, *in* childhood. I recognised you, Father, in the stiffness of the sheet your foot would never throw off, and it was the same fear that my life had already opened to and would disappear into, like the River Foulou swallowed by the sea.

I recall that other death, beating in the most tangible of life's hearts, in the most tormented living flesh, that wrenches you from yourself, from all your dreams, from all your meaningless broodings, from what we call childhood, from all-consuming terror, that pushed my father to give me my husband.

A name for each secret, for each wound, a name for you, for each of your faces, I call, I recall, an image that echoes each name that answers, like the voice of Father Delanoé who had agreed, at my request, to come from Yaoundé to Obala on the day of the funeral to give the absolutions of the dead. From prayer to prayer I call, I recall the notes of the requiem as, uninterrupted, they rang out. The solid presence of pain, the long attachment rent asunder, lingered and intensified during the final prayer around the deceased that Father Delanoé had consented to recite even though my father was not a Christian and had always refused to convert.

Memory's barbs bring back my father's image and with it all the reasons to love less, to revolt, to almost hate and have it rooted more deeply, more firmly in me.

There were times, I admit, when my own faith wavered. I confessed this to Father Delanoé, the sweat of anxiety when all to which I tried to cling, deserted me; when, awake in the middle of the night, there was nothing in front of me but the reflection of decomposition, the grave the village idiot had dug and the stench already of decay.

I knew his whole body would one day crumble and vanish. I knew nothing would remain, that it would rot stinking in the earth, death having seized, kneaded, broken it up – a bluish memory beside the grave. But the physical body matters less than the things that survive; the soul of the deceased that leaves the world of men for the world of the dead.

Then came the time of the day when the villagers, surrounded by the elders and witchdoctors, formed a shape like the kernel of a strange fruit; a condensed memory, garnered in these beliefs and religions, and as though buried in its sharp, passionate and enigmatic language. The guardians of the ceremony, the witchdoctors, of whom Mamie Titi was the mother, encircled this incombustible centre that was like a vase brimming with flavours, scents and light. A warm maternal mantle radiated from Ma, her mortal coil, in which the other celebrants, dazzling in their blue *gandourahs*, could sleep and dream.

Heads in hands, the group of witchdoctors swayed slightly and sang, their voices touched by the solemnity of the ceremony – a discordant and mysterious chant that perhaps only the bird bearer of souls could understand.

To the officiants it was a unique moment – the foundations of the earth, the forest where the souls of the forebears dwelt, Father Delanoé mesmerised by the strange ritual, the witchdoctors moving to their breathy visceral song. The family of the deceased and all the villagers, led by Mamie Titi, were infused with a desire to accompany my father on his nine-year initiatory journey from the corruption of the earth to his eternal abode.

The crowd of stragglers at the back of the procession, silent at first then whispering, made their final tour of the village before regrouping around the coffin to make their way to my father's house, with its high mud walls flanked by mango trees, at the foot of which my father's body would be buried.

My thoughts strayed to the other side of the journey that Mamie Titi had so often described, the crossing of the River of Spirits on the wings of the bird bearer of souls or in the belly of the pilot-snake, the arrival in the eternal world where the elect wait.

Broken up by coconut palms and mango trees, and gouged with deep lines, the landscape was a permanent delight. The mugginess of equatorial thickets gave way to the relative cool of twilight, and it was an exhilarating moment when the proudest of the villagers removed their sandals and wiggled their toes, and when the witchdoctors, now freed from care, took off their blood-red fezzes on Ma's instructions and chanted elegantly and softly. The intoxicating libations and chanting grew louder, pulsing in manly breasts.

I took advantage of this blissful interlude to look at Ma and drew her into my musings. Fascinated by the radiant face overseeing the ceremony, like the face of the first woman I ever saw, I began to wonder, so unwavering was her appearance, whether her healing powers had not sent her out of herself and into a state of saintliness so that the negation of the flesh could take place.

I knew fear was rife, since no one had been found guilty of my father's death, and I was also convinced that behind and deeply embedded in this fear lurked a very different feeling, one that would remain hidden and mysterious.

When the power of imagination became almost unbearable, everyone – with a precision so horrific that each trembled, that each heart skipped a beat – saw the finger of suspicion point to him. However, something in me resisted the destructive nature of the fever, the panic threatening to swamp me and, my eyes fixed on Ma, I found in my stilled heart, in my breathlessness, an inexhaustible source of happiness.

15: Ma Disappears

▼

The day following Father Delanoé's departure, the landscape around Ma's hut was as though mineralised. Petrified were the stiffened leaves of the coconut palms drenched with native, musk-scented night, the dank smell that the earth-washed bark released into the acid cool that exuded an occasional sharp peppery bouquet.

A long guttural cry suddenly rent the forest; but for its violence, it could have been mistaken for a death rattle. The woodpigeon's cry flashed through the sky then came back to Ma's hut, lacerated my body and carved its scratches in me. It settled on the deserted track where the euphorbia clung to its silence, to the leaden stillness of the landscape.

My fear having subsided, I was rapt by the transformation, by the entwining of black stiffness, by the fetid, water- and earth-saturated air reminiscent of the smell of the grave.

My soul was bewildered. Something had passed over the landscape leaving it parched and sterile – an evil breath – but where had it come from?

A deadly desolation had suddenly descended, and the spongy earth was now rigid, hard. All that could be seen – the remains forever encrusted – were roots, creepers, vestiges of greenery and calcified deposits. Because the earth had become illegible and had only this petrified memory to offer, all I could do was wander from fault to scree slopes with the bitter taste of dereliction in my mouth.

Thunder had rumbled for the best part of the night.

The storm had unleashed itself, filling nature with rage.

I must have paused for a moment and leant against the trunk of the tree Ma loved to sit under and stared at the brown coconut lying in the grass. The sight of it broke my heart. What an excruciating ordeal! Ma's whole life suddenly flashed before my eyes! And with it the same suspense, the same unbearable stab in my breast, as clear, as perfect as the coconut.

▼

Was it real, this vision of the old lady alone at the back of the hut open to the four cardinal points, collecting splashes of sunlight, listening to her two woodpigeons whispering secrets in her ear?

And those half-dreamed images of Ma at the foot of her tree, surrounded by the insects she'd named, electing roots as a haven of grace – that is what permanently glorified my reverie.

The bark of the coconut palm at the foot of which she loved to sit had a silky feel, evoking a mother's tenderness; the loose bark allowed the finger to sink in and stroke it, to strip away the strands. The coconut palm goes back to the shores of creation; it watches over the dead and nourishes the living.

With her incoherent prophesies, between flashes of lightning, her incomprehensible stories, frozen beneath the coconut palm bearer of souls, Ma took the form of an oracle. I am like those old men who eagerly search the shadows for a buried song that they think they are about to capture but which constantly eludes them.

I ran to the four-door hut. A flash of pain suddenly appeared and illuminated me. Ma had disappeared.

The raffia curtain, one minute slightly raised and the next, the clear inflexible silhouette had left the world, awakening in me a whole theatre of shadows whose projections would only end with my life since after all these years they still continue to parade before my eyes.

How could I contain memory's muddy waters? How could I break, save with my last breath, the ingenious jinx? It was as though, unable to tear myself from these memories, from the sight of Ma taking her snake-bird bone flute from her haversack to become absorbed in sounds strange to me, I would never be forgiven for not having fully grasped the beauty of the lyrebird. For so long believed to be the seat of salvation and success, the song took away my pain, and without my realising it, comforted me. The magic of the music stripped away the scar of childhood, unfolding the damp sheets in which I would be reborn in the arms of Ma.

As a mother takes a child to her breast, so the flute took its notes to God. I, who for so long had expected everything to come from my husband rather than from this strange distant melody, whose quiet restlessness I had refused to hear, how could I be in any doubt that Ma, seated under the immemorial coconut palm, her two woodpigeons on her shoulders, had been the harbinger of the nocturnal visitation that had guided my life for years and enfolded me in a shroud of reminiscences?

Nothing came to me but from this music. It alone did I inhabit, like light during an eclipse; by it alone was I haunted.

The villagers were upset by Ma's disappearance. So great was their pain I knew I would remember their distress for a long time to come, and that I would feel it as keenly, and with the same gasp they had given when a woman rolled on the ground in a fit of convulsions, when a man in a Terylene suit chanted that the guilty party was no longer among them. As for me, I vowed to find the guilty one, to unearth the truth, even if this elicited from me the starkness of a cry or a farewell. I vowed I would travel the length and breadth of the countryside, that I would question old men, and if need be consult with witchdoctors.

Each day I journey deeper down the vale of memory. On my guard against their whims and metamorphoses, I seek the images that the guardian of life was always offering me: the memory of Ma with her two woodpigeons, the clatter of pebbles in the courtyard, the creepers so black and so bare.

On impulse I murmur, 'Ma'; the fetishism attached to her nickname lives on and the pleasure of uttering the voiceless syllable takes me back and, fingers trembling in the daylight, it's as though I'm opening her blue robe, touching her skin still soft despite her age and more radiant than the long translucent folds of sky or light that cover her, and burying myself in her breasts.

No one knew where Ma came from or where the shadow she was seeking or fleeing originated.

Although vivid, the images I had of her had rejected or transformed her many faces.

Pain obliterates everything. All I could see was the rent that shattered the healer's many names, the wound that stopped my breath, my feeling of oneness with the essential flow, eyes open, my capitulation to the dull tedium of life.

I shall never know why Father Delanoé refused to share Ma's last meal with her.

Could Mamie Titi's eyes, like the crucible of God's light, see what others did not?

My body surrendered to the blows that rained down and stabbed right through me. For some reason I kept visualising the sacrificed mother mourned by the two woodpigeons whose cries mingled with those of the grieving crowd in blue.

How could I have known, after this incurable grief, that the dead woman's silence was a word frozen in my mouth?

There were times when I found myself imagining I was the child she'd never had and that she would carry me inside her beyond death. I was coming to the painful injunction, against which I was still rebelling; I would take my godmother's suffering upon myself. The illusion lingered, obliterating all others – I would experience the disintegration of her self, identify with her loss and embrace her death.

16: Witchdoctors

▼

And so Ma had left our world. She had left her hut open to the four winds, never to return and, apart from her image that lives on in me, I knew I would never see her again.

Ma, her unforgettable disappearance, my last meal with her, the sense of unease she'd left me with – I could still picture all these in my mind, but I would be quite incapable of describing Ma herself, apart from her ebony radiance, her unique beauty – fiery and sad, voluptuous and melancholic. I found her extremely beautiful, and was struck by the classical purity and joy of her features.

If, every now and then, I recall the turbulent times when I consulted witchdoctors in the hope of meeting Mamie Titi's successor, I do so not out of nostalgia, but with a smile, a touch of tenderness and compassion.

When I think of witchdoctors, it is Souleyman's face I see – the long plaited hair, broken nose, jet-black eyes. I picture him sitting on a chair by the fire in the courtyard, a ghostly figure, vulnerable in the forgetful memory of the living.

The wind carries away the image of the witchdoctor's acolyte: the necklaces, the cowries crossed over his naked chest, the white outfit with the twirling fringes, the pale kaolin streaks on his entranced face, and the blood-red splash of his headgear, the insignia of senior initiates. I felt vaguely disturbed as I recalled how witchdoctors rise at midnight and at four in the morning to carry out their ritual ablutions with bark from the raffia, a magical tree with the power to heal, for their skins must never come into contact with water. The linear patterns cut into the skin were enigmatic symbols only understood by horses.

During the rainy season, night falls so early – at five or earlier on a dull day – that it's necessary to illuminate the area around the caravanserai. The witch-doctor was in fact the only one to own a hurricane lamp, which gave out a pale glow. Adolescents, all of whom were firstborn males and potential initiates, would offer him matches. Like the other visitors, I, solemn, rapt, watched the paraffin's whispering ascent, the incandescence of the blackened wick from which the weak flame rose dramatically, the same golden yellow the sun sometimes has when, at the height of the dry season, it settles on a thatch roof between two mounds of earth.

I watched this new shade of a more watery, more pale, more translucent white than that of a flame lit from within. I could hear the paraffin's mysterious murmur as it fed the blade of fire; I revelled in this, the luminous feast that is always so strange and so moving to us Africans.

That night, as the sombre light hadn't filled me with as many strange sensations as it could have done; the moment the last onlooker had left, I returned to watch its renaissance, as though the flame's exhilarating ascent could bring me back a mother's joy. I was so heartbroken by the absence of my firstborn whom tradition had taken from me. Staring at the hissing hurricane lamp I stood riveted to the image of the abduction as if it had only just happened. Every now and then, the dreamlike slowness of a gesture made it burn brighter.

This moment of intense joy, had I not experienced it at least once before with the child that heaven had sent me, only to take him away from me? The unwavering brilliance of my love for Douo lasted five years.

Had the wheel of happiness stopped turning? And the wonder of motherhood that I had believed was eternal, was it forever shattered into memory, was it watered by the same love, smothered by the same tender golden embraces? At any given moment I could summon this image, and with increasing regularity I turned towards what had survived adversity, towards bliss, whiteness and sun, where my untamed, innocent love lived on.

Weary the future, and weary and ruined the rapture of maternal love. Misfortune had caught up with me, outstripped me, submerged me.

I watched the witchdoctor sitting on a sculpted wooden seat, supported by the bird and the serpent, the long black veils of the visiting women, the knotted trunk of the mystical tree, the lamp that burned white, the only one left in the village, come from a world troubled by adversity and affliction.

Did I need to be staring misfortune in the face, to be completely lost to have come to consult Mamie Titi's successor in the hope of finding my child, to entrust the future to this ambiguous shadow with his necklace of amulets which were like as many imaginary roots linking him to the spirits?

I needed a land where I could breathe, a person to whom I could turn, the lost paradise I had helped create. And it was still to my child that I reached out. I would have loved to carry him away with me.

That is what drove me to Soulé, to the edge of the working-class areas of Essos – a buried memory, passion and absence linked, and this organic rebellion against sacrifice. What was I hoping for? To be delivered of memory's whisper calling inside me? To have got as far as Essos was to be as close as possible to the wound, to feel its gaping; to secure, as it were, the lost child in the distance, whose name, whose tender, whose cruel and agonising embrace I re-enacted before going to sleep.

17: Magic

▼

The spirits who lurk in tangles of roots and creepers are not the benevolent spirits of the righteous, but the evil, demonic spirits of those who haunt sorcerers' noisy gatherings. Just to think of them makes me infinitely sad.

I feel a crushing, compelling longing for soggy, black matter; to be submerged, to dissolve like the marshlands opening beneath my feet, like the viscous abyssal holes, its mud pregnant with evil spells. Whether you take one step forward or remain still, evil holds you in its supernatural grip. Wild lush nature is its grinning sceptre. Plants spattered with dark stains, ferocious animals, monsters that dwell in the forest, the forbidding watchfulness of sticky moist trunks, reptiles with malevolent bellies and breasts, reawaken the cursed kingdom of idols.

Evil powers passed through Mamie Titi and left her unscathed. Inside and all around she saw the misshapen; she'd run, collapse, she was the rent that took away the world. Penniless, she lived a life of abandonment, of restless wandering, of perdition; she was swept away like a leaf. A dark core formed around her, a thick impenetrable armour of life.

The time will come when, like her, women will assert themselves by rejecting marriage and motherhood and the tradition that insists that a woman on her own is like a broken vase. Ma's revolt made her a mythical and respected figure whose unpredictable nature would one day be made clear to me.

Tonight I question myself again and tell myself –

or do I just want to find some crazy similarities I could be cultivating – that if the image I have of Mamie Titi is so strong, as if some mysterious aura had emanated from her the moment I sat down opposite her at the rattan table in the cobbled-together hut where she held her consultations, it was obviously because the images – her dancing shadow on the walls of the hut, her unapproachable superior presence, shapeless and nameless – were linked. And it strikes me that this link, this strange connection, did not come only from the recollection of my first consultation with the healer. The reason that Ma's image appeared at that precise moment and in that very place was that it was connected to the turmoil of one particular night – one single night that was the mother of all nights – the extreme closeness of the pain that came when I was reminded of the loss of my child.

A shadow brushed past me. An extraordinary dark power loomed over the mother of witchdoctors as I wondered if I would ever see Douo again. Before day had properly dawned, night was dispersed by the first plaintive cries of the woodpigeons. And I, the little sacrificed goat now baptised, watched Ma as she moaned softly. When she spoke, I felt the bright waters of hope rise in my heart. 'My successor will tell you how to find your child. All I can tell you is that you will meet someone who will change your life.'

For a long time I remembered that I'd consulted Ma for the sole purpose of finding a new food that would release me from time and transport me to the voluptuousness of dreams.

In the presence of Ma, nature became the visible manifestation of the bowels of the earth; her motherly affection anticipated the wishes of the world and made them come true in the hereafter. The world overflowed with its bliss.

I now recognised the forest as the real absolute, the *here* that needed no elsewhere. I who had left Obala for Yaoundé and thereby widened my choice, picked it to be my infinite homeland. It had taught me how to look and sharpened my senses; it was all things unto itself, it nourished body and soul, and was filled with meaning.

A land free of irregularities or imperfections surrounded Ma's hut; a calm space, the new magic of a universe destined to decay. A harsher, less cumbersome land. Ma's predications came disguised as allegorical discourses where parable and myth alternated in a style not unlike that of the *griot*. They were more or less the sum total of her knowledge and she drew on them as one would a repertoire of stories and fables. Although I never grasped the full meaning of her words, I learned that the physical world was not the whole world, and that the supernatural order of things and of life was more real than the commonplace.

Ma told the story that when Zamba, the Lord shaper of souls, first conceived of mankind, he created man and woman. With his eternal breath and word, Eden was made. Then he blew on the man and the woman and bestowed upon them seven paths to knowledge: two ears, two eyes, two nostrils, but only one mouth. May the whole world fear Zamba, God shaper of souls, may all the inhabitants of the earth fear him, for when he spoke everything was born! Thus spake Zamba: 'From your mouth will come a doubled-edge tongue with which to bless or curse, but you must only use it for good.'

Eden reflected the glory of Zamba, and luxuriance communicated the work of his breath. The eternal sent man and woman into Eden and left there a lizard to be the guardian of their actions.

They hadn't long been in the garden, when the man flew into a rage, thus defiling the garden of delights. Beauty burned like stubble and perfection withered as his curses rained down.

The hand of Zamba summoned woman and man. Their accomplice, the lizard, went down to the marshland and washed his mouth and ears to forget everything he had heard. However the curse rose up from the earth and echoed to the edges of the world.

'How great is their sin!' Zamba exclaimed. 'I shall go down to earth to see if the exclamation that rises up to me did indeed come from them.'

Man and lizard denied the evil they had done. Woman took the blame upon herself. 'For pity's sake, let not the wrath of the Creator be provoked. I shall confess.'

Thus spake Zamba. 'A curse on you, lizard! Because you lied, you will forever be deaf and dumb. Through man who lied death will come, and as for you, woman, who likes to take the blame for something you did not do, I will give you two extra paths to knowledge, two breasts with which you will initiate men into life. Their tongues will thus open up to the glory of the Eternal.'

All the stories told me by Ma felt like scarifications carved into my skin to radiate the secret of our origins, silent for so long. And today, my father dead, my child lost, as though pushed to the limits of myself, as though seared by the secret, I return to them.

No longer carried by the same momentum that had taken me back to my father's house in Obala, to the radiant sacrificed days of my early life – and it wasn't just the memory of my earlier bewilderment, the cuts, the scars – my lips were shut tight so that nothing could escape, so that no one would know of my pain.

What a long time it would take for the wound to heal, for the pain to subside!

▼

My father was dead and many months had passed. I no longer went to Obala. There were no more stops, no more trips in bush-taxis, no more striding through the forest, and inside me the secrets that would knot and unknot when I came into contact with Ma. My injured motherhood has never stopped tormenting me. Mamie Titi was the only person who could bring me peace.

I cherished Ma after Douo disappeared, with genuine maternal affection. But it wasn't the hibiscus, the shade or leaves of the mangrove, the tall, poised golden stems of the sunflower I had to contend with, nor the murmur or frequent strange *whoosh* of the barn owl, the echo of his flight through the air, but *the loss* – how can I avoid saying it? – that had reduced me to nothing.

I remember those evenings when Ma received those who sought peace. And I haven't forgotten the sacrificial feast she offered those who came to consult her, as a pledge that they would be healed. I recalled the guinea fowl cooked in its skin, the unusual aromatic presence that brought on a kind of rapture. I felt dizzy, suddenly strange. What was it about this water fowl on its bed of banana leaves and coarse salt that made it smell so good, with its fatty flesh and skilfully stitched skin, when Ma pushed it, studded with garlic, hot pepper and mint, into the glowing embers?

I was interested to know whether Father Delanoé had noticed my reaction when he announced he was leaving Yaoundé to pursue his apostolic mission in Douala. It was only much later that it struck me as odd that the Father, during his visit, had refused to come and share our meal.

I shan't forget the long discussion he and Mamie Titi had and, try as I might, whenever I look back, I still can't imagine what they had to say to one another about the previous day's ceremony in the healer's yard, to which I had not been invited. I'd felt left out.

It was a crazy sight, Ma in her blue robe, standing to kiss the Father as they made their farewells. Indelibly imprinted in me, trembling it surfaces now through my bitter tears, through the moon's pale and steady glow.

And why was Father Delanoé – or did I imagine it – embarrassed?

Though he returned Ma's kiss – indeed it is unusual in Africa for a woman to take the initiative in this situation – his discomfiture was unmistakable.

18: Terror

▼

I arrived in Essos as day was drawing to a close. It was the same shimmering night of my dreams where the sun unfurled only to break on the first crescent of the moon. Born at the top of the hill, the crepuscular ray ran down the raffia roof, then a streak on the sea enveloped in one fell swoop the solid gold of the monkey puzzle trees and the call to the dead; and the spectacular aria, as if pulverised by the light in the furnace of late afternoon, blazed around Soulé's face.

Seeing the light curl towards the oblique and magical crescent of the moon, I felt a pure water well up inside me and recited a peculiar dark lesson.

The visitors formed a circle around the witchdoctor, their eyes fixed on Soulé's slightly bowed head, which was all that stood out against the background of woolly green vegetation where the souls of our forebears were held captive. The same magic held everyone spellbound in front of the solar figure dedicated to the brightness and to the night of their pains.

Then: the words, their union, their elation or defeat, between the spirits and ourselves, the perplexing frontier, imagination's quivering flights. A mature woman was suffering from crippling headaches. She described a pain of old that still tormented her. Was it normal to suffer so? Was it not abnormal to probe the suffering, to brood over it like a custard-apple, wondering how to reach it?

It was time to speak, to tell, for Soulé was a good listener. Nothing moved him more than the plaintive cry or breath of people flowing through him; when they couldn't take it any more, they spoke to him, they told him everything. The healer still wasn't used to the fact that he could help others with a sign, some advice, a word, a hand reaching out.

During the day, but more so at night, I couldn't stop my thoughts from straying to the witchdoctor's closed room. Inside I had seen with terrifying clarity, a row of male caiman tails hanging down, and the bark of the *okubaka* that retained as intensely, as powerfully, the tree's alarming mythical ability to be invisible and to keep enemies at bay. At first I slowed down, then shivering, uneasy, I moved quickly away from the wall of the hut and managed to avoid glimpsing it.

There was something deeply disturbing about the prospect of drinking a calabash of fresh blood, of having vampire-owl feathers brush my naked face, and mingled with my fear of death was a wish to penetrate the secrets of the here and now and the elsewhere. There was no doubting that I was absolutely terrified of spending the night on a bed of fox-bat bones, but beyond and within this fear, a very different feeling was also emerging.

Whenever my powers of imagination became too much for me, I'd reason with myself to dispel my fears. I had to convince myself that however disturbing I found Soulé's attributes, only they could help me find my child. For there was something inside me resisting the panic that threatened to return, and which found, in my trembling and anxiety, in this unshakeable nest of magic, an inexhaustible source of hope.

Did I think the consultation would bring me the same peace and serenity I had experienced in Yaoundé when I used to cross the forest to visit the mother of witchdoctors? Would I be content to secretly nurture, to breathe in a trance, the hope of finding my child? How the phrase floated up inside me, how beguiling it was, the pledge that I would be healed. Try as I might to forget the sharp and painful stab, my child's bewildered face the day the nuns came to fetch him, the look he gave me that forever encapsulates him, the anxious image of Douo which, everywhere, and at all times, returns to haunt me.

Discreet though they were, the witchdoctor's young male assistants, all potential initiates I would only meet once – but long enough to remember their swarthy scarified complexions, their naked henna-streaked torsos – were there, I was sure, to change and steer my future. I was unaffected by the way the hut seemed to contract and hold us huddled around the sacred fire, having grown up in a small town like Obala where the bush invaded from all sides – under the windows of our huts, the monkey puzzle tree with its shaggy branches, the River Foulou in the distance, the valleys, fields and orchards, reflected even in the heat of the flames that split it – and experienced no deeper nor more moving union than with the discordant chants of Soulé and his assistants that contrasted sharply with the melodious song of the lyrebird.

Unconsciously, emotion crept inside me, a hazardous ferment that would rise only later. For where else would the feeling of wonderment have come that beat in my heart whenever I thought of the pink and grey flash of the two woodpigeons as they soared above Ma's hut, of the white mark of their wings and streaks of their necks, their looping flight as they skimmed the waters, the too swiftly carried away rhythm of the snake-bird bone flute that had exploded in my face?

Thinking about it again, I would have liked to sink into joy, to wallow in it, to lose myself in it.

Soulé was unavailable or more often than not absent, busy searching the markets and bars of Yaoundé for clients. People knew he was in when they spied his staff, a true baton of office, surmounted by a baboon's skull, streaked with two purplish-blue chevrons to symbolise his occult powers, which, adding to his standing, made him even more unusual, more fascinating.

I concentrated on remaining calm. I had panicked earlier after having taken only a few sips of the decoction of *eboka* (the bark with a thousand properties from which the rite takes its name) one of the assistants had handed me, after they and Soulé had drunk of it.

I was terrified when I thought I heard myself gasp, and my heart missed a beat when, from the straw mattress where I lay, I looked up and saw long threads of drool hanging from the lips of the healer and his assistants.

I paused and entrusted myself to the *eboka* rite. Was it this madness, this aberration, that I had secretly sought? I was reassured by this hallucinatory manifestation, this discordant rhythm that I thought I could get my breath to copy, that I thought would regulate my heartbeat until I could reconnect with the presence of the ancestors and learn the truth about our origins?

Fettered for so long, I had to rein myself in, keep myself on a leash; was I really that frightened? Finally

I had to let go, give way to emotion, lose myself and free myself from myself. I doubted I'd make it to the end.

What did I fear, what panic did I want to overcome, which was reining me in again, binding me? That inner voice for so long stifled and now fighting back – was it mine? And was it what I wanted, at all costs, to suppress?

And then I heard a voice, the one just risen inside me, or Soulé's? I knew not. It said, 'Before the white man can give you back your child, you must bring me one whose cord that binds him to the bowels of the earth has not been cut.'

19: The *Eboka* Rite: The Opening of the Inner Eye

▼

Tears fill the dawn and the sky comes to sit on the sand. Silence penetrates the mass of the darkness. The *eboka* rite is about to begin.

Blinded by tears, it is with the new eyes that open inside me that I lean over my vision and contemplate it. So this is it, the *eboka* rite, the opening of the inner eye, the split, the sudden distancing from pain and like an icy game with memory. In the glow of daybreak, I see a long orange streak slide over the town; it rumbles, fans out in the open air as far as the horizon. The azure is darkened by night's bites; howls of rage pour out and fill the sky. A veil of lassitude spreads over the plain and sends back the crash of thunder, flashes of lightning and tremors.

I touch the back of the image. All that remains is her, she of the seven faces, on whom all greedy eyes are fixed. Confusion overcome, all that is left is a painful smile, detached from all violence, from all grievances. A face eaten by the void. The unavowable creeps into the secret chambers of death like nocturnal beings waking in the night.

When truth becomes public, many men put out their eyes; others are swallowed by the abyss of shadows, while others, without stepping over the edge of the world, make their way to the ancestors' promise of morning. To shut themselves in a spellbinding, near-ecstatic silence, they have torn down the vapours of dawn.

With the clatter of tom-toms, the humus returns to

its mineral stiffness. Behind the woman with the two woodpigeons, there stands a man with an angry frown; his eyes burn with melancholy. 'She holds the keys of death and of the house of spirits!' the stranger yells. Is he black or white? I don't know. Through the *eboka* vapours I feel only his hatred.

Then the ground begins to quake. I see a crystal ocean studded with fire. One last time the false healers worship their idols. The evil spirits are thrown into the sulphur-fuelled river. Eaten by ulcers, poisoned, burned, crushed, blaspheming the men die, refusing to look at the woman. They are vanquished and stung by a shower of hailstones. Even the birds feast on their rotting carcasses. I see the souls of those who have suffered the axe. Night and day they are tortured from eternity to eternity.

Night falls and terror sucks the life out of them. And all this time the infernal eye sparkles. Like a sated animal the town curls up to sleep, now nothing but a whore who feasts on blood.

The town drinks hungrily from the dark river of intoxication. For a long time to come the town will bear the scars of its pleasures; voracity will alternate with mortification until they share each day, the one returning to drive the other away, as punctual as misfortune.

The woman gestures and all the men kneel around the hut open to the four winds. The bizarre stranger follows her like her shadow. She blesses him, reciting incantations that the assistants repeat. She holds a coconut palm leaf, charged with the abundance of her grace. The stranger sings the healer's chant. When it's time for benediction the woman turns towards him. She prays for her sins and that her wishes be heard in the ancestors' heaven.

The setting sun lights up the blue moon. The song of the lyrebird soars and immediately dies.

Now that the countdown to peace has begun, the woman officiates alone outside the four-door hut. She strikes her two woodpigeons with her forehead. Lying prostrate, she is beyond the reach of prying eyes, impervious to unhealthy emotions.

Silence descends on the pacified town. The prayers of the redeemed rise in the ripples of the river. The woman has regained her original brightness; her strength restrained or released, her pulsing, her natural rhythm, all the yearning that allows the gods to shine among men.

Laid bare in front of him, the man sees the secrets of her heart. The woman's face reveals them to him before she leads him to the spring of life. I see an immortal flame leap from the man's eyes. His smile raises the woman to heaven. I see the blue moon again; the two woodpigeons soar into the sky. Standing in the water, the man speaks in an unfamiliar tongue. The woman follows him, plunges him nine times into the fire of the river and then disappears.

20: Deliverance

▼

As I emerged from the hallucination, I wondered why I'd let myself get involved in the mystery of *eboka*. Why had the visions rooted me to the spot for so long? I had always been fascinated by the *eboka* rite because of its evocative, visionary powers and its suggestion of physical corruption – the rolling eyes, drooling lips, convulsions. I was enthralled, too, by the almost carnal intoxication that inspired a sense of the world's symbolic death, an abandonment, a dispossession I might never be able to quell.

Paradoxically, when Soulé enjoined me to find a man whose cord that bound him to the bowels of the earth had not been cut, my delirium left me, and the procrastination over which I had brooded for so long, was showing me another conjuration of Mamie Titi's disappearance. I kept returning to the same question: who was the man I had seen next to Ma and who had precipitated her disappearance? Was he the successor to the mother of witchdoctors? I had been given a journey to complete even though all I would take with me was the answer to Ma's disappearance.

Was it so stupid to have thought Soulé was Ma's successor; she, the mythical figure who was to haunt me for months? But having wanted it to be so for a long time, this was the myth onto which I held. It was as if another person had supplanted Ma, as if a man could supplant the mother of witchdoctors.

Needless to say, and as though my need had come out of nowhere, I had to continue on my journey right to the end, and maybe go to Douala where

Father Delanoé had gone, a fact corroborated by rumour.

I could no longer ignore something that was becoming increasingly clear to me, and would have to accept the idea, but not without a twinge of sorrow and deep-seated revolt: the Father had set himself up as a healer – he whose fascination with Ma had been, to say the least, ambiguous and tinged with dislike.

I hadn't completed my search; my fumbling questioning of those who had an extra eye led me to take the train from Yaoundé to Douala.

My terror would for a long time be linked to the visit I paid Father Delanoé. The mystery which I felt surrounded him was never completely dispelled. It was always with the same curiosity that I recalled the Father, smoking a cigar from the mountains of West Cameroon while the native witchdoctors chewed tobacco.

The image of the Catholic mission in the Bali area of Douala, whose doors were always open, was older still. It was there, in a round room – the oratory – that the Father recorded the dates and events in his life that had led him to call himself a traditional practitioner rather than a healer. But what had given him the right to espouse the strange powers he was alleged to oppose?

The Father's soft voice brought me comfort; my pulse stopped racing and my breathing settled down at the thought of the white priest and the sparkling billows of hope he inspired in me.

What a lot of memories, fears and anxieties he was able to dispel as though that was all my life had been. Now that his eyes had been opened, now that he had glimpsed the other world, become master of the night – was he frightened of himself, of the hereafter he had tamed? As if powerless to move, stand, smile or kneel on a prie-dieu, holding a half-smoked cigar he'd never finish or flick the ash from, he talked to me as he read an antiphon from his breviary, open in front of him.

This same prie-dieu, a symbol of Catholicism like the icon on the wall depicting the Child Jesus on His mother's lap, bleeding from the crown of thorns, belonged to another universe, one I could neither join nor inhabit.

Deliverance, liberation – did I think they would come from this brush with spirituality? Would my child be held prisoner in the bottomless pit into which I had plummeted, inside which I wanted to shut myself and remain, not moving, not breathing, as if in some joyous realisation of motherhood?

I didn't invent the Father's insistent words – 'the answer lies within you; you wouldn't be searching for it if you hadn't already found it' – nor did I imagine the starry eyes that stared at me, and from which I couldn't tear myself; I who was stuck in the past, in those five years of happiness, in memory's musings. Like a blind man I grope, searching for the lost child's face, alarmed at the chasms opening up before me, at the pit into which we'd slipped.

So incongruous was my yearning, deeply embedded in emotions and regrets, that for a moment I thought I'd dreamed I'd visited Father Delanoé. And yet, everything had happened as I remembered it, the clatter of pebbles in the courtyard that hot muggy night. My only regret was that the mango tree was so bare that as I passed I saw no fleeting shadow of a fruit on its parched skeleton.

I was probably conscious of my strange gait, but the ground – of pure sensation and emotion – on which I trod had brought back the past. What turmoil I was thrown into by this difficult return! If only the wound had never existed or if only it had closed up: healed. Forgotten, it certainly was not, and it was this wound that was reopened by the pus of the past that I had welcomed with such trembling pain.

I was permanently in a state verging on terror, surprised to find myself more often than not disconnected from both present time and place. Recollections of love came to me, of the joy of motherhood – the silhouette of the child leaning against my breast, a large banana leaf in the forest, my grandfather's rocking chair – images as memorable as they were insignificant.

All I had to do was dig deeper inside myself. I had always been guilty, guilty of being a mother, a woman, of having abandoned Ma. *Guilty of being*. Could I have changed and saved myself?

21: Journey to the Island of Malimba

▼

The day following my consultation with Father Delanoé I left Bali and went to Bépanda to catch the Doula–Edéa train that would take me to the Island of Malimba where my Aunt Petronilla lived. Malimba lies in the Atlantic Ocean to the south of Douala and is the island paradise home of the spoonbilled ibis.

The sense of confusion that impeded me so was intact and still held me as intensely and as tightly in its mystical grip. Imagine my horror then when, in the New-Bell area between Bali and Bépanda, I saw – his face all swollen, the liquid blue from the blows spreading over his cheek and down to his chin in a pool that was slowly turning black – a man who'd been beaten to death. The ghastly corpse of the stranger – the crowd had the right to remove the penis of its victims – had attracted my attention, not only because of his black eyes and broken body, but also because I thought voodoo magic was involved. A sorcerer can put a curse on someone at the request of a man who wants to be rid of a rival in love by having him deprived of his virility.

Fear and death intermingled. Is it not always the case that we are frightened of death? Is superstition not a fear of death that can suddenly, whenever we are confronted by our weaknesses, make us feel that it is close enough to touch? Each time I recall New-Bell, that same anguish returns.

What I wanted from this visit to my aunt on the Island of Malimba was to fleetingly but intensely possess the spiritual world of nature, and at the same time to have the possessing of it wiped from my memory.

During the hour-long train journey, I recollect my cry of wonder at the blue flash of the hummingbird suddenly rising up out of a burned meadow dotted with shrivelled grass in a loop of the River Sanaga, the kingfishers skimming the waters, the path edged with broom whose whiteness exploded in my face. How I would have loved to enter, alive, the fusion of sun and memory, to bathe therein and become one with it.

▼

From the train, I watched for the first scattering of huts in the fields, then, the moment they had disappeared, the cross of the chapel of Edéa.

To reach Mouanko, where I would catch the ferry to the Island of Malimba, the train ran alongside Lake Ossa, only visible through the trees first thing in the morning or at dusk, when a milky streak announced its presence. Through the window, halfway between heaven and earth, you could see the lake's arm like a watery bed, a smear, an inert reflection.

Getting out when the train stopped in Edéa, brought me back to the here and now. I stepped on roads I haven't trodden since, and will never again tread except in dreams. It isn't so much the stop I remember but the oldest of images, the one of my son, emerging from the abstract distance where he was buried, to inhabit night's unrivalled beauty, to fall asleep with me to the song of the weaverbirds.

There was something special about the quality of the light and I found my country's sky deeply moving.

The light made me conscious of an order of truth where things are neither themselves nor the reflection of themselves; rather they flee and fade into a myriad of fleeting significances.

It would take too long to describe how each feature of the landscape – rubber tree plantations, palm groves, fields as far as the eye could see – was sucked into itself and disappeared to leave no other trace but the scent of tears. Ever since, I have blindly sought it again.

Time slowed down but my longing was greater, more solitary; and I realised I never reached out for anything nor for anyone, save my lost child.

In my silent union with the African landscape, Douo appeared from the most deeply hidden of my desires, and unresisting unfolded before me, while my flesh sank into the peace of the world, at last acknowledged, accepted, embraced.

My recollections and longings had emptied me. Also, as a result of the *eboka* rite, I was experiencing a sense of physical dispossession. The feelings that persisted for my lost child didn't strike me as strange but deeply familiar. Absence, now manifest, was the consequence of my firstborn having been sacrificed and the fact that I had been plunged into a state of unlimited availability by his abduction.

22: Union with the Island of Malimba

▼

I arrived in Mouanko with the first song of the weaverbirds and took the ferry for the Island of Malimba. This clearly delineated space, this narrow entrenchment is a miniature version of Cameroon, a precious haven full of amazing things. To visit it is to be filled with a joy that some travel great distances to find.

The Island of Malimba rightly claims its translucency is better than any other; it is a pungent translucency where the spirit can delight in just the grain of the light.

The landscape is sufficient unto the day. There are times when I dream of crossing valleys and lagoons to commit to memory each port; for we know only too well when we cross these beds of solitude, how the invisible eludes us.

Slow like the island but open to different meditations, the sea flows around the Island of Malimba.

The day I arrived, the surface of the sea was taut with shadow, and the silent forest had frozen in the wake of a hurricane. And yet they say that when the weather is bad the water can turn green, reflecting the colour of the mangroves growing out of the bowels of the earth. During the dry season, when the sea breeze blows across the island, iridescent patches can suddenly appear in the imperial green. The deep, translucent colour is that of an emerald or some other gem evoked by the island inhabitants.

The Island of Malimba – Aunt Petronilla had known it all her life. Having been born there, she knew the land was magic, a carrier of light. My gaze would stray like hers, idly taking in my surroundings, noting the fragments of cassava leaves, lapis lazuli patches that caught my eye. As I climbed the hill to my aunt's hut, bits of the sea disappeared.

The sea! It didn't matter whether you could see it or not; in fact, it would have been better, up there on the plateau, for it to have been but a dream so you could smell only the prison of palm tree branches.

So many secrets were locked into the familiar climb to Aunt Petronilla's hut, into walks exploring the sky. Maybe from up there, if I took the time to stop, I would see the sea. From the top of a seemingly endless sky, eddies continually battered the Island of Malimba, and here and there a huge swell would lift foaming reefs that sputtered in the shapeless bay. Shimmering with humidity, the island blew its own breath to meet the sea. Whichever way you turned you felt you were breathing water.

The day after the hurricane, it was a dazzling liquid sky that rose to greet me, shrunk to a soft sheer fabric. A vibrant light infused each tree, every leaf on the pandanaceae with breath-taking freshness. The sky slowly condensed into it, and I felt I was moving towards it, arms wide open, until I too was this melancholic blue, this heaving wave whose momentum froze when the storm died down.

The silence was woven with the faintest of sounds; the random songs of Gabon parrots, the vibrations of the hibiscus, the rustlings of green mambas, small snakes with a painful bite.

Hearing the sighs of the sea, I felt safe and sound, for a while at least.

When I reached Aunt Petronilla's hut, a sparrow

hawk called out and all of a sudden an infinity of jubilant, gleeful birdsong exploded all around. The warning had sounded: in the tall wilting grass, in the gritty scented dust, there lurked a green mamba.

I stopped as another thought struck me. The island was suffused in a silent, unfathomable mystery and the miracle that was uncovered made it a garden of delights. A paradise of light and dark, where the nearby henhouse would light up while the banana plantation next to it slipped into the shade to hide.

Above Aunt Petronilla's hut, the cocoa plantations reached to touch the horizon and would send back the magic of whatever pulsed in the distance. It was the hour of the day when green woodpeckers sang themselves hoarse. My aunt showed no surprise as I greeted her, 'Good day, Aunt Petronilla.'

'Where on earth did you spring from?'

'Don't you recognise me? I'm Ékéla, your brother's daughter.'

'My, haven't you grown! And what brings you to see your old aunt?'

'I've come to ask you for a goat to offer in sacrifice.'

'Poor Ékéla, I don't keep goats any more. Three moons ago, the sorcerer, Olende, sent his hyenas to eat my flock. But let's see if my neighbour Zoe can give you a goat.'

I turned to look at Aunt Petronilla's garden. The goat pen was empty. All that was left were a few ropes lying on the ground among the tufts of grass. The guava trees were in a different place, and I might have thought my memory was playing tricks on me had my aunt not explained that she'd had them transplanted to speed up the harvest.

I never knew why, but during my visit to the

island, I rediscovered my love of the land.

Sky and sea had cast their spell on the Island of Malimba. But another kindness was bestowed from above, the mango trees, those wonderful mango trees. Whether they formed a green knot in the middle of the forest or grew in a garden, they beckoned the traveller.

Emerald green, purplish brown, leaves dotted bright red, so many precious fragments embedded in the landscape.

In this country, only ferns, citronella, raffia palms and sisal trees suddenly spring from the soil. The joy of this island is that there is no landscape without trees, no landscape without momentum. On this side of the island, nature grows wild. Tall grasses have rolled into the foreground; peonies and ivy weave their foliage around a kapok tree.

In the nearest hut, made of adobe, under the shelter of huge baobab trees, a group of villagers were gathered around my aunt's neighbour. It was she I would visit later that beautiful hot day, before following my heart back to Father Delanoé accompanied by the sacrificial animal.

23: Initiation

▼

Back in Douala at last, I stood outside the convent whose doors were always open. I raised my eyes in the direction of the Father's oratory, for that was where I would find deliverance, where I would soon be embarking on the long, painstaking work on myself, from which I felt I might not emerge intact.

So vivid was the memory of the day I offered Father Delanoé the little goat reared on the Island of Malimba that I would never forget it.

Humble though the offering was, it nevertheless indicated I was asking the Father to intercede with the spirits on my behalf. Could he devote himself entirely to the task without being distracted, not even for a second? I told myself that the witchdoctor would have engaged in mysterious exchanges similar to those that came to him when he was in a trance and the ancestors appeared to him, as he endeavoured not to lose touch with reality, as he smoked the old cigar he'd lit that would just go out.

Eyes focused on what was beyond the world, the Father waited for nightfall and for convent life to slow down; and for that to happen he had to stop living, to put his life on hold, for he knew his visions would only connect, would only have meaning through the negation of his own identity.

That night I felt no greater nor more moving fusion than with the stone walls of the convent sweating in the stifling tropical heat, than with the knotted trunks of the mango trees and the heady scents that disfigured the air.

Terror struck deep within me when I saw young Nganga, the apprentice witchdoctor who assisted Father Delanoé during the ritual ceremonies. I remember the bleating of the goat as the witchdoctor put drops in its eyes so the animal would open the way for the green decoction, extract of seven barks, with which he would anoint my fontanel.

I realised possession was but a leap, the abandonment of a drifting body, the extinguishing of the fretfulness of the soul.

I didn't know Father Delanoé but I was wary of him. I knew nothing. There had always been a wall separating me from everything. I was a secret to all mortals, except perhaps to my lost child, and later to Mamie Titi. I'd never seen any of them open like a drop of water exploding in the sun, like a chestnut burr forsaken by its fruit.

Tremors, dispossession, the feeling of initiatory ecstasy that accompanies the rite to lift a curse – these were not what I sought as I stood beside the grave the young apprentice had dug for me in the convent courtyard. I would have to lie inside it nine times, like a stoat burrowing in the snow, to await a death. In this solemn game, I would have to parody.

And if I had the impression I was participating in a mystery, in a sacred ritual, it was never more so than when the Father placed on my abdomen the trussed-up goat, infused with the fragrant blue mist of incense. Then I waited for the sacrificial victim to at last reveal the mysterious route that would lead me to Douo.

From the hole in which I lay, I raised my eyes, then closed and opened them again. I could see the two of them; the tall, slim, young black apprentice, so unassuming, come early to the job, instantly obeying Father Delanoé's commands. The white witchdoctor was corpulent; in Africa his bald patch signified a split, even demonic personality.

Images! More images! My memory proceeded thus; each tiny little detail as clear, as sharp as a pain – of the crucifix above my head, the seed belt that was Father Delanoé's stole being waved around, the obscene lines of young Nganga's scarifications.

All these images pestered me with their yearnings, as did the stabbing pain that bore deep into my heart when first the witchdoctor then the apprentice blew on my head, then raised to my lips the earth that would make me fertile, and which connected me to the land of our forebears.

Images! Always images! Why had it taken me so long to realise I had gone to consult the Father in order to reconnect with life itself, to be reconciled with my rebel memory that gripped my longing ever tighter, and which was telling me I had to let go, to calm down.

24: News of Douo

▼

I had to go back to Yaoundé. I left Father Delanoé but not without a pang of sadness. Then there was the stop at Eséka station, on the Transcam 1 line that goes from Doula to Yaoundé. There was nothing left to solicit. Should I set off in search of nothing or the impossible?

Had I never lost anything, except my child? So why did my hands feel this empty, not only of what I had once held, but also of what I had briefly coveted, of the fleeting sensations which, unnoticed by me, one day passed through me, like bream passes through the smooth waters of the River Libamba?

The fact that I had once experienced this emotion meant I was able to recover it intact.

I think only I could have experienced that nagging but baffling sense of embarrassment, of joy, when the train stopped in the middle of a night no different from any other, at Eséka station during the three-hundred-kilometre journey from Doula to Yaoundé.

I only ever saw the huge station at dusk, and was beginning to wonder whether light ever found its way in. Moreover, probably because of the burial mounds erected outside the doors of the houses and the fact that it was a starless night, it felt like I was in an underground passage, a catacomb, a labyrinth dug in the foundations of some buried temple not unlike the graves that were lined up in front of the dwellings to prevent sorcerers from stealing the souls of the dead.

Eséka station could be called oppressive and yet it was almost comforting.

Hour after hour chimed. The stop in Eséka was like a midway point that heralded the beginning of the second half of the journey. There was still a long way to go; many kilometres, many hours, yet the promise that we would eventually arrive never faded.

But I had my doubts. Maybe we'd never reach Yaoundé. After all, we'd been travelling for hours without seeing the sun rise. We might carry on sinking deeper into darkness in this tunnel of time into which, unbeknownst to us, we must have strayed and from which we might never emerge, forever stuck in the night, forever prisoners of the rusty carriages that might never again arrive anywhere.

The rhythm of the train had changed; it controlled this other rhythm inside me, the gathering momentum or deceleration of the movement, to which, part grateful, part alarmed, I had surrendered since our departure.

At a less breathless but bumpier pace, the train cut through the dense vegetation. On either side lay open, ashy or scorched valleys, where dwarf palms or rubber trees clung; as well as wooded outcrops and patches of green where, here and there, hunters' villages appeared alongside brick-red, laterite tracks. I found them enthralling, and it was the same dream or obsession maybe that returned whenever I saw these oneiric landscapes.

I will arrive. I did arrive. The hunters would be there on the platform. I'd know them by their tall black silhouettes, their grim expressions and the guileless glints in the liquid ebony of their eyes; and all around, there would be the pungent smell of meat on smouldering embers.

And it was there that I encountered and became one with the image of the traveller. I was both in and outside it; fusing and at the same time pulling back. I was part of the festive atmosphere, and with an aloofness that was also involvement, communion, a sweet and burning closeness, I contemplated the freely flowing palm wine, the distilled alcohol being illegally sold in the carriages.

A good-humoured cacophony filled the compartment. Bright red, yellow and orange fattening pens, seldom seen in the countryside, reached as far as the carriages, in tightly packed rows like cows in a stable that looked more like grotesque insects with their metallic carcasses. Inside, hidden from view, were the goats, sheep and chickens vying with each other with their bleating and cackling.

When the train was about to gather momentum for its steep and rapid climb, I turned away from the menagerie, shut my eyes and prayed to God it didn't portend a derailment.

Yaoundé and yet not Yaoundé. It would only be Yaoundé up there at the top of the hills. And in a way, you had to earn it, to deserve it, with that extra wait, a protracted longing, a final test.

Here is Yaoundé's first hill. We slow down for the climb. To the left, the coast the train has just joined. We are now running alongside the crossing track, spotted with dry yellowing green moss, the humid brown of mushrooms. Here and there grass grows up through the cracks of stones and along the track prickly nettles so painful to the touch.

So that I would forget nothing of a journey where I had breathed, happy – and, dispossessed mother that I was, because I had to endure gazing alone at places and objects that reminded me without returning him to me of the child whose eyes had so often looked at them – I watched over, I reopened the wound.

▼

I wanted to see my terror through to the end; maybe it was already beginning to crack on account of the doubts I was having which were as painful to me as the heartbreaking scene I kept picturing, of me sobbing over the dead child in my arms. I thought of those elephants who, it is said, lie next to their dead young and stay there until they too, trembling and numb, can at last pitch into the same night.

Sometimes I ask myself whether I was only ever filled with wonder but by the vestige left in me – which, the more it faded the sharper it grew, and which I sought in the lost child – of our shared nostalgia, that quiet inferno, that glowing beacon off the coast of our lives.

As I got off the train, the convent bursar handed me a letter from Douala. I read the words, the ones that leaped out at me, the ones that steeled my heart, sometimes surprising me, annoying me, the ones which, so long awaited, I'd had to tear from the gangue of swarming silence. My fear returned and I rose up against the alarming complaisance I intuited between the lines when the Mother Superior informed me that Douo had adapted well to European-style life.

I felt the words might shatter, might scatter, might fall apart under the pressure I feared I could no longer contain. I told myself it had nothing to do with the plea, the longing, my uncomprehending passion had inflamed. This was not the end I had anticipated when I embarked on the journey that had led me from Soulé to Father Delanoé. Peace, or at the very least a respite was what I had sought, for I had no other haven to turn to the way I had once turned, albeit in vain, to life and normality, to family life, to motherhood.

The surge within me would subside of its own accord, delaying for a moment the violent onslaught. Was it for this that I had embarked on the journey? To read this letter. To say farewell to the oppressive present.

25: Meditation

▼

On my return to Yaoundé, I wanted as far as possible to limit my contact with my husband's other wives, to retreat from words, from repeated gestures. I was blind to the haste, the intensity of the gestures of these women who were closer to my mother in age than me.

The rivalries, the need to be assertive, to dominate, to possess, all the energy crystallised around sexual power – all this was still alien to me. I refused to be like them, to join them in their power struggles.

It seemed that the bizarre events that had precipitated my adventure, the quest for a man whose cord that bound him to the bowels of the earth had not been cut, heralded a different, more vertiginous order of things and pitched my life into a state of renunciation.

I never imagined that one day, through a reversal that was not of my making, my life would turn into a spiritual experience and that as a consequence my injured motherhood, which had until then held me rooted in the elementary, would become less of a burden and less intrusive.

That I would never find the man bound to the other-world, that the ground disappeared beneath my feet, that the contours of objects blurred, all these things originated from the same obscure, silent roots. As though I'd been alerted to the illusory nature of my quest, it was with a tranquil heart that I embraced destiny's promises like as many lessons of the night. Others have said the same of salvation.

Although they had found it they still looked for it; although they'd already been saved they wearied themselves searching.

I spent a long time looking at my life, at the void that defined it, searching, trying in the absence of an ever more absent heart, to identify with it, unite with it – to know at last who I was in the here and now and the future. All of a sudden I realised my existence had abandoned me, that I was standing at its edge, as if above an abyss that was enticing me, sucking me in.

The hollowing-out process was extremely slow, outside time almost, and this gradual decomposition of matter to the point when it finally disintegrated, was an infinite inner experience. The void appeared suddenly at the heart of my universe and revealed that my life had been naught but a dream.

My experience of things whose very foundations had been undermined, exposed the vanity of the world. Up until then, I had believed motherhood would be the fulfilment of my expectations. But now that the dream had been shattered, hope was greater and more alone than ever and focused on nothing but the renunciation of motherhood, which, with unlimited insatiability, kept it connected to itself.

Try as I might, no call, no shout to the lost child would cross the threshold of my mouth; I had become the body of my grief. Never had a pain brought me closer to myself. It was with a bitter kind of joy that I reiterated that thought the night I allowed myself a respite.

Unaware of what was happening inside me, this lull was a revelation; not an extraordinary revelation of which I was unworthy, but one that cast a new light on me as a woman excluded from the world and from motherhood, and on a destiny possessed by a spurned splendour.

I clung to the memory of Douo's birth like one who, on the brink of acute pain, focuses on a pointless activity. My attachment to the painful memory of the birth in the blue shade of the solitary sisal was what stopped me from going mad. I concentrated on committing to memory every last detail of the delivery – the cord that bound him to the bowels of the hereafter I myself had cut, the inner tearing, the primal scream that had everything of a deliverance about it – a grotesque process compared to what was happening in the labyrinth of the other world.

I was on my back, eyes shut, hands on heart; happy, in a new and stable temporality, to be present at this my waking dream. I was familiarising myself with images of silence, of solitude, my earlier anxiety quelled, evaporated into an altered view of the world. In the dark lucidity where the soul's bliss is barely freed from sleep, I was blessed by the night, no longer anything but night itself imparting its knowledge to me. My senses woke to the physical reality of the world and I was filled with gratitude.

Was I so different from the child I had lost? My resentment became what it had always been – the mirror of myself. I remembered Douo; the sky's gaze haunted by his image. For the first time I was able to feel the happy coinciding of present reality and reminiscence. I was nearing the moment when the foundations of identity and time would vanish. Maybe the uniqueness and strangeness of the event was but a new and original aspect of earlier reflections, in whose impenetrability memory was taking root?

26: Apparitions

▼

Only once did I return to Yaoundé to measure the pain Ma was causing me.

I was a woman eroded by absence, and also a woman, in appearance only, with a family, a husband, responsibilities, and who, ever faster, was rushing to look at her life. Naïve icons depicting apparitions of the Virgin Mary, who might exist in all of us, lay in secret wait. I dared not raise my eyes to the voices that kept me bowed in devotion. I sensed this though I didn't want to see it, though it might have been what I wanted above all else to see. I was woken by the mildness of the night, stricken by a need to speak, to taste the passion with which these unknown voices that left me on the brink of tears were bringing me closer to myself.

Then it was that a strange, rather terrifying figure appeared to me. She, whose face was suffused with night's glow, a melancholy being who at first reminded me of a Virgin who knew all about suffering. I felt the blinding sweetness of her gaze upon me and something gentle filled my mouth. All but spent by the final metamorphosis, I was reduced to a patient, pleading soul at the threshold of the darkest of raptures. Then it was I caught sight of Mamie Titi's shroud and felt my body separate from me. I cut deep into the scream, but the soul's shrieks are all alike. Truth alone tears us asunder.

The Virgin wore death's face. Of God she had kept only the black sun, from where she would rise from absence. Apprehensive, petrified, my gaze wanted to touch, to possess this body and its soul and dissolve therein and merge with its beauty.

I might not have been so enamoured of her whiteness had so much darkness not emanated from her.

Then she vanished. I was horror-struck as though I'd suddenly discovered I was without a heart or hands. Abandoned naked to the light, I fell upon the spot where her feet had stood, telling myself over and again that this time I really was dead.

These apparitions shed their light in me as I slowly rediscovered the meaning of timeless gestures. For the moment I should like to describe once and for all, the world I was in, as I reached out beyond expressible grief, to acceptance, to acquiescence to life – which is to acknowledge absence – to the root of all love.

The things that occupied space and defined my life were one by one affected. Like an immaculate canker, reminiscences were burrowing deeper down, and it seemed that memory would devour itself and leave no trace.

The world – or rather that part which immediately surrounded me and which I considered to be the world – was becoming one with memory's aura. Once they'd been touched by it, the dreariest of activities dissolved, disintegrated, disconnected from necessity, disappeared. Having abandoned all attempts to find an explanation, I lost my predilection for images, the meanings of words.

What desire wanted, in its hollow immobility, what desire had *always* wanted and awaited, was the end of signs, the removal of tension and for the self to disappear *into* the self – a primary invagination in the cradle of unconsciousness.

Desire was the ultimate mother; like Ma it reigned by virtue of its pure opalescence. Every now and again, and as though a flash of lightning had suddenly appeared in me to illuminate my own darkness, I told myself that because of the misfortunes of my race, I had mistakenly bracketed together death and guilt.

Born and formed in wickedness, my story had become rooted in error. The wound of motherhood, far from bringing me the fulfilment of womanhood, had been a punishment, a mortal chasm to which I aspired; and I felt a growing desire to really *be* in order *to no longer be*.

27: Great-Uncle Pantaléon's Second Funeral

▼

Not long after my return to Yaoundé my Great-uncle Pantaléon's second funeral took place. This was the rite of the second funeral, the rite observed nine years after the first to mark the culmination of the spirit of the departed's journey in the belly of the pilot-snake or on the wings of the bird bearer of souls from the corrupted earth to the everlasting world of the ancestors.

Where was I to find the comforting balm of memory? The veil had scarcely been lifted and there, dead these nine years, was my great-uncle's silhouette refusing, like all wise men, to stare at the horizon, head between his knees, and view the world in its true nature.

How was I to suspend the reversibility of time, how was I to lift, if not with my last breath, the contemptible yet magnificent spell? Memory sank its fangs into me as the smell of the bloody trail of the sacrificed cat whose heart had been ripped out and given to the village headman, returned. We dared not be moved by the animal's fate as the witchdoctor rubbed his fingers before reading the entrails of the feline whose unseen presence accompanied the ancestors on their journey to the hereafter.

Fretful and torn, I wanted to remember every last detail, to miss nothing of the funeral feast whose smoke nourished our forebears, of the tom-toms' mournful voice as it drifted between sorrow and longing and released the words of the dead.

The village headman and notables dropped by – I knew them all. They weren't wearing the blue or gold loincloths with the cetonia sheen they donned on important occasions; just plain grey suits and brightly coloured feathers in their hair.

The village children walked in step, in front of the headman, from door to door, in response to the voice of the tom-toms that rose like grain in flight. And I, what I expected from the promise in the muted pulse, what I listened for in the distance, were troubled tom-toms, then a minute of terrifying silence during which the solemn procession would greet the notables at the foundation stone that had witnessed the birth of the village, near the hut of the dead. What I dreaded was the visible manifestation of the sacred, the hollow horns and subdued frenzy suddenly rent by the death rattle of the sacrificed cat; a more insistent note, like that of the bell to the dead that unsettled the soul.

The world was not the ceremony I had taken it to be and the people weren't officiant-laureates, destined to celebrate it. The arcane voices of the tom-toms rang out in the dark just as Great-uncle Pantaléon, dead these nine years, was about to progress from being a buried corpse to being a name as permanent as eternity.

I told myself that my great-uncle was buried with his head pointing to the ocean beyond which lies the land of the dead, unlike the village's founding forebear who was buried with his eyes fixed on the bush. My great-uncle, I told myself, just like my father in under nine years, will be reunited with the clan of the patriarchs. I turned the words over again and again, like a calabash in my hands. I opened them, examined them, delved deep into them, in search of my great-uncle's image and the image of his skull that the village bachelors would take from the grave near where my father lay, and then cover with a white then blue cloth, before the village filed past it to acknowledge his departure for the hereafter.

Vanished, gone was my great-uncle's dark presence in the whitened sepulchre. In the dying day, it seemed to me that a huge skull which grew larger with each step it took, was making its solitary way through the huts; its brightness filled the village, like the mounting sobs in the house of the departed that reached out as far as the shrine.

But the glorious shimmering sun was swallowed up as though carried away by the muffled beat of the tom-toms, and as both moved away, a very different feeling – painful, rebellious – welled up and supplanted the image of the unearthed skull on which the sacrificed cat's blood had been poured.

Any minute now, as if death had never been in the world, there would be the lilt of the tom-tom under the window of the hut, the door would fly open and there in the frame would be my great-uncle's ghost, taller than he'd ever been, even at my wedding when he stood up and raised his arms to bless me as the benzoin fumes burned the bright colours of his bubu. I no longer saw him as my father's brother but as a traveller returning home.

Of all my memories, this one came flooding back to me from out of the heart of the village. And I trembled as if I'd never left the hut, as if I'd never, not for a single day, stopped seeing, over and over again, the spectacle of the cruel rite of the second funeral in the room of echoes in which I'd shut myself. I'd left behind the ghastly scene of the decomposition, but the tom-toms, intensified by the widows' wails, continued to vibrate inside me. The rhythm seemed to accelerate in response to some breathless impatience inside me.

Then came the slow processions, one following the other without a pause; one had already gone to the shrine when the next appeared. From the side, where the first coconut palms stirred, came the urgent tread of soldiers in safari jackets; in a khaki-clad parade of jerky steps and gestures, they came and paid their final respects to one of their own.

The officers were there, beneath the tent. I knew them by their tall dark silhouettes that stuck out above the others. My eyes met those of Emmanuel, his liquid ebony eyes almost too clear, and in them was, I swear, a light; and as I looked at him, I swore again that I would never allow it to go out.

As I stood next to the officers who'd come to pay their respects to an old soldier, the long tresses I'd untied were flowing down my cheeks and one leg was bent in a dance pose. I was struck by how much Emmanuel resembled the Sénoufo mask I'd seen in Father Delanoë's oratory. I had always had a predilection for looking at African sculpture, seeing in it reflections of reality as well as the distinctive features of the faces around us – hence the wooden mask with its high cheekbones and slanting eyebrows, the gash of the lips, the rounded nose and penetrating eyes.

Emmanuel was watching me. I saw a section of the mask in his face and body and his likeness to the sculpture endowed him with a beauty that made him dearer still. Haunted by uncertainty, haunted by insufferable tensions and, whether near or far from them, haunted by the expectations of my family, I wondered whether I was a woman he could desire, whether the man watching me could transport my image to the world of dreams, which up until then I had been unable to penetrate.

My physical appearance probably confirmed any misgivings he had regarding the beauty of my face – the imperfections of my skin, my tired cheeks, my body, the clod that weighed heavy on my soul – and tempered his desire. I, on the other hand, was convinced it would be no bad thing to sacrifice my life to the unique masterpiece, the rare paradigm I was contemplating.

Desire is not enough for someone who believes in omens, who can read only them and for whom the truth of a feeling has only ever emerged in the radiance of a gaze or the quiver of a lip.

Who did I love? Did I really love this person? Was it the man with that face or was it the mask, the expression, the promise I thought I could discern in the person that resembled the mask?

All it took was a memory, an empathy for me to be drawn to this work of art. Everything originated in the physical presence of the Sénoufo mask. The image that offset the desire of the flesh brought with it the promise of peace.

28: Emmanuel

▼

One day in May I walked into the officers' mess where Emmanuel was waiting for me. The sweetest and happiest of smiles lit up his face when he saw me. We were soon chatting more freely and easily than I ever did with my husband. How great had been my disappointment when no feeling of any kind, no obvious or deadly passion had developed between my husband and myself; how upset I'd been as I waited in vain for the magic to develop. With Emmanuel, it was as if we'd always known one another, so there were no barriers, and any embarrassment soon vanished.

With this man I had no need to lie. I was indebted to him for playing a role, and for appearing to be connected to my childhood, to have emerged from it as from the magnolia blossom that bloomed white in avenue de l'Indépendance in Yaoundé.

I gave up trying to rationalise and surrendered instead to my dream, accepting the almost tangible certainty telling me that once given, Emmanuel would not take himself back, that his manly body would protect me and that, once open, his pure but passionate heart would never close up but would be mine for ever.

I needed love to be a refuge, a security; I wanted it to be a body and heart finally breathing in unison, to find the bliss my husband had been unable to give me. Only Emmanuel, I sensed, would endow me with the feeling of completeness I sought, and only with him would I experience the ecstasy, the miraculous harmony.

How could I endure my marriage, the events that had sidetracked my life, the wrench from the green paradise of my childhood in which I had thought I was forever rooted?

Miraculous month of May when for the first time I discovered what love was! There were no tensions or misgivings, no regret or remorse, only a flourishing and a joyfulness. While I was bathed in this whiteness, filled with a sense of harmony and completeness, I wasn't to know that nothing would ensue from these moments. However, no one can take them from me and maybe all I need do is remove their invisible cover to see them shine brightly again?

It is Emmanuel I address, to him that I murmur my memories, him that I urge like a cry for help to also remember, not so I can stop time and return to the warmth of our meeting, as if in the meantime nothing had happened, nothing had changed or eclipsed him in any way, but so I could relive it, so I could once again feel the essential tenderness of a love that was still with us, which in a flash, in an instant, could reveal itself to us, which was perchance waiting for us to save it from oblivion.

Body and heart were one. The most sensual of loves is also the most tender, the most innocent. Innocent was the communion whispered to our bodies, innocent too was our wonderment, whether on a street corner or in the officers' mess when, happy, impatient and excited, a rush of adoration would have us trembling.

This passion, this culmination for which I had yearned, and which my marriage had served only to intensify, smouldered deep within me. The vital source of our love was the only place in the world where I felt free, fulfilled and alive.

Probably since childhood, certainly since the wrench that had brought me to Yaoundé, I had only ever aspired to feeling secure. All my fears, all my misgivings stemmed from having been reduced to the status of a slave by my new family. I had thought I had a sense of being rooted, if not of permanence, when I was growing up in Obala, when, by the light of the moon, my grandfather would tell my sister and me the founding myths of our tribe; and much later too, during those precarious moments of happiness when Mamie Titi sang flanked by her two wood-pigeons.

I don't think I had ever felt as secure in myself or known such bliss before, not even as a result of my deeply moving meeting with Ma.

Emmanuel's love made me whole and brought me peace. He was able to free me of the terrible emptiness into which I was always in danger of plummeting. Everything about Emmanuel became a symbol of my fulfilment, of my elation; I loved his scent, which was a subtle blend of vanilla and incense, I loved his Air Force uniform.

In all these demonstrations of love, there was something intrinsically connected to the very essence of his being, to his noble and proud bearing that I admired. But this prevented me from seeing an aspect of my passion that belonged to a less obvious impulse: it was as if desire itself had become the language of revolt and as if my soul needed to rebel and dispossess itself for another.

29: Passion

▼

A quarter of an hour before I had to leave for home, Emmanuel would drag me into the shadows of an alcove, where we'd be like a couple of youngsters hungry for a few moments of privacy together. It was impossible to tear myself away from Emmanuel, to leave him and return to my life as a recluse – never to breathe him again, never to impregnate my body with his smell and his heat – and, as I walked down avenue de l'Indépendance, drunk on his scent, the touch of his body, I was enveloped in my ache for him. Would Emmanuel transform the fundamental uncertainties that had remained hidden since my marriage and take them to another level?

Whenever I feared I might never be able to express my freedom, it was those same doubts, the same visceral anxiety that surfaced; body, desire, marriage, motherhood – all these were but an excuse so that I might hide and reappear in a new unanticipated and unstoppable form.

My self-doubt might not have undermined me so, I might even have been able to overcome it, had it not been exacerbated by some kind of shame, of confusion that had driven me – like a hedgehog rolling into a ball – into a retreat from which I thought I would never emerge. Nothing had been able to obliterate all traces of the rupture in my life.

Whilst I believed I loved Emmanuel, and whilst, albeit briefly, I even contemplated starting a new life with him, this was perhaps because he embodied the habitable part of the world, the freedom that had one day been taken from me. I felt the same whenever I read the Bible Father Delanoé had given me the day I was baptised. The Samaritan woman's cry of amazement at Jacob's well, I made it mine; I pleaded with God – as though this were still possible, as though if time were abolished we could start all over again – to intercede, to unite the hearts of all, the fathers with the children, my husband's with Douo's.

Had I reread the Gospels, I might have taken on the characteristics of the Samarian woman; Emmanuel was the incarnation of God and of He who asked the woman to slake his thirst.

We are not guided by our thoughts. It is our internal agitation, our memories, the confused inner murmurs we are scarcely aware of that allow our thoughts to fool us as they do.

My meetings with Emmanuel were always filled with emotion and wonder at the warmth of our passion, but they were occasionally marred by worries or anxieties. Can night's powers ever be welcome? But my inner turmoil – what was it, compared to the elation I felt, the desire I'd discovered in the innermost tremors of another's body?

I was filled with the blissful sensation of a breath swelling my breast, as well as remorse and the shard of anguish that pierced my heart, whenever it crossed my mind that, like the Samaritan woman, my frozen life was haunted by a nameless, a nagging threat.

Emmanuel and I lived love blind; he, locked into what had become everything to him, his passion for me, and I, wandering aimlessly and slowly away from him.

With a mixture of curiosity and dread, I waited for the images of revolt and fantasies of freedom I'd carried around since childhood – garnered from the Canon Crapon's version of the Bible that Father Delanoé had given me and through which I'd leafed so often – to come to life.

I recalled some of the icons in the cardinal-red Holy book, which replaced the more traditional religious images. Oppressive and in a way inspiring, paintings like Veronese's *Moses Rescued from the Waters* exuded a bluish grace and Raphael's *Betrothal of the Virgin* a reddish beauty, in which even a layperson like me could discern a poetry, a melancholic love pledged to a higher destiny.

I waited for revolt to revive other images, glimpsed or intuited, and bring them to life. I waited for revolt to fill me again with the sense of horror and strangeness Rembrandt's *Struggle between Jacob and the Angel* had stirred when I first saw it. Here, confrontation exposed desire's burning barb. I saw the suffering of the world multiplied tenfold, drawn-out, so raw I felt both within and without what a monstrous presence freedom was.

However, the image I remember thinking prefigured the feeling I was waiting to engulf me, was a detail in Rembrandt's *The Denial of St Peter*. Surrounded by soldiers, the apostle's pained and hostile expression had filled me with the same unease, the same anguish and suppressed terror that I could read on the faces of the men waiting in a frozen huddle in the olive-green light of an eerie background.

I – a girl of the night, a catechumen come late to baptism – wanted to glimpse this hidden horror, this sacred terror, so that I would know how it suddenly surfaced, how I could seize the secret of this otherness.

30: The Scene

▼

I could never recall Emmanuel without experiencing a sense of bewilderment and a deep-rooted awe that would bring a lump to my throat. But that evening, as I went home to my husband, a very different feeling overcame me. I suddenly felt alienated, cut off from this passion. I might never again – all atremble – be able to approach a face like Emmanuel's which now seemed a great distance away.

That evening, the impression was especially acute. With it came a sense of resentment against men. I felt there would always be this distance, this alienation between them and me, between life and me, between the beauty I couldn't relinquish but which filled me with sadness, and the horror of the abduction that had deprived me of my firstborn.

But I was also riddled with guilt because I felt I could so easily have levelled my criticisms of men at myself; and that if there was this distance between Emmanuel and me, I had created it to forestall life and had used my marriage as an excuse to avoid giving free rein to my passion.

My husband was waiting for me – frozen, tense. The silence between us deepened. I must say something, I must explain why I'm late, I thought, but I was so stunned by this hieratic, self-absorbed figure, that I couldn't say a word.

'Where have you been?'

'In the fields.'

'In your town clothes! I might look like a stupid locust but you can't fool me with your lies. My other wives tell me you haven't been going to the fields; that you disappear for days on end like the chameleon in the sand. Swear by Zamba that you are and always will be faithful to the shadow of my shadow. Swear that your body will never surrender its secrets to anyone but to he who was the first to know it.'

'I never swear, but standing before the mountain I look myself in the eye.' I felt humiliated. Nothing felt more undeserved than this humiliation. And it wasn't me I reproached but my husband and any man who demanded I explain myself.

There were other, more violent scenes with the other wives. He beat Emilia when she returned late from the village fête and slapped Anaba's face because his tobacco wasn't dry enough. There were long days of silence, his face cold and hostile, when I forgot it was my turn to do the washing.

I am like the gazelle, I am able to talk but prefer to remain silent so as not to attract his wrath.

My humiliation, and probably the realisation that I was neglecting my husband, must have had some bearing on the satisfaction I derived from the fit of jealousy I'd provoked. I was no longer the nothing, the anonymous wisp of straw I'd been in Obala; at last I existed in my husband's eyes, and his sudden interest in me, these early stirrings of feelings were enough to win me over.

Satisfaction was soon replaced by stupor. The shackles seemed at long last to be coming undone and I felt there was once again a place for me in my family. However, I was also aware that if my husband had made a scene it was in order to assert his power or to influence me by going so far as to model his behaviour on my father's.

My passion for Emmanuel had made me sensitive to the impact of the environment, the atmosphere that was forcing my husband to make the gestures we wanted him to make, to become the one we wanted him to be, for submission and bending to the lowliest of tasks, humility and fidelity were considered to be woman's natural attributes.

The ivy had barricaded the shutters; to open the window you had to tear down the suckers. Bits of beaten earth fell away. When I went into the kitchen the smell of tar hit me. I looked up and saw the trickles that sealed up the chinks in the corrugated iron that was our roof. A weary bat crashed into the cracked wall; underfoot the crunch of dead desert locusts. Before turning around, my eyes strayed into the yard, to the *mvout* tree, whose fruit turned women's lips red, to the avocado trees growing next to the henhouse with its ill-fitting doors, to my husband's hut; and I was filled with a longing, as breathtaking as the serene flight of dragonflies in the sky, for things to return to normal.

The rattan table was covered with a film of groundnut oil. More than anything else, I needed to sit and think; to let my hand wander over the tabletop, in search of some imperceptible yet present thing. I was reconnected, with what or with whom I couldn't say, but the sensation was there, new and comforting.

31: The Brother I Never Had

▼

Was it because of my father's ardent desire to have a son that I, no less passionately, used to long for a brother?

If I think of this now, it is to ask myself why my father, who'd never had a son, had wanted to make men of us, making us feel we were an accident of birth and that we'd just have to make the best of the situation.

I don't have the wherewithal to expunge this failure, this sorrow, nor am I able to accept it as such. I had dreamed of sharing the love bestowed on me and of giving the one who loved me another being other than me to love. Handsome and strong, I would have wished him to be a bit rough. I wouldn't have been jealous of my younger brother, for I was sure he would have loved me as much as I loved him.

There were times when my sister Thècle and I complained about being mere girls, and while we weren't aware we lacked anything, we already in fact lacked everything. Incensed one day, Thècle told me she thought the dear Lord was the devil!

Our accursed womanhood had us trapped in an image with which we were forced to identify ourselves by those around us, although our goodness was in part able to make up for this outrage. We couldn't accept that God would have created second-class individuals and just abandoned them to a life that was taking place outside them.

It was up to us to free ourselves from the mortal skin our father had wrapped around us. Our eyes, possessed by the sleep of the dead, wanted to smash the misfortune of being women, the tragic and brutal blindness that kept us isolated from the world.

I liked to imagine my brother suddenly giving me a passionate and despondent hug then, without taking his eyes off me, and shaking his head violently from side to side, backing away through the hollyhocks into infinite stillness.

For a long while I imagined my childhood had been different, infused with the same sensitivity, but made-up and as it were parallel to the one I was living. The dream was pure fantasy, vanishing the moment it was born, and if I am describing it now, with such painful abandon, it is because it beat with the same heart-rending hope of suddenly recapturing the richness of my life – in order this time to guarantee it and perchance save myself.

I wondered, had I had a brother, what extraordinary love and openness there might have been between us.

Not so long ago, this dream, like a shining arrow of light, had cut through the gloom of being a woman, and had given rise to a hopeless and overwhelming desire that I still associate with the memory of the coconut tart as it appeared to me, inviolate, in Mamie Titi's hut.

Had I not experienced moments of pure bliss, which came one after another without interruption, at least once with Emmanuel, and not in the flashes of my imagination, but in the world? I knew too that that still and radiant eternity was also the incredible experience of my love for Douo, our five-year-long whispered union, not an iota of the memory of which had been altered. And although I hadn't been aware of it, this reminiscing had for a long time been as essential to me as sweeping landscapes or street sounds are to others.

This fidelity to my innermost aspiration brought me peace and was my only chance of happiness.

Slowly, with my growing maturity, the world began to change. I witnessed the transformation and observed the variations of light and shade and felt myself at last *become* – without ever ceasing to be what I was. I felt at one with the daylight, and through the kitchen window that the sky managed to penetrate, I counted among the simple pleasures of which I never wearied, the shifting light and darkness that suffused my space.

There were staggeringly beautiful moments when the melding of the different golds and dark reds touched Yaoundé's seven hills, which quivered and twitched like the happy flesh of a newborn baby.

32: The Pilgrimage

▼

Having decided to return to Mamie Titi's village, sorrow hand in hand with death welled up inside me, and all of a sudden I knew from the way my heart stood still that Ma would never come back. Today, I draw up an inventory, not just of her possessions, but of all the sentiments, sensations and memories I associate with the hut open to the four winds.

Didn't I know the second I looked away from the abandoned bird-bone flute and its magical power that magic and fear were not to be found in objects, were not to be found in the world?

On the whole, it was never during the day, but only at night that I felt fretful in the hut, and my fear wasn't just of the dark. I associated the hollow space in the bamboo bed with Ma's disappearance. I was in no doubt that there was a close connection between the dip hollowed out by Ma's body and her being spirited away.

It is said that spirits sometimes leave the mark of their passing on a pebble or wall. This was similar, except that it wasn't the spirits who'd left the indelible mark. Perhaps it was death.

In the half-light, I glimpsed the basket where she sometimes kept fruit, especially mangoes; their fragrance perfumed the air and still lingered in the room several days later. I remembered the dishes she loved to prepare – the familiar dessert of coconut tart and the crunchy smell like glazed honey as it cooked in its earthenware dish. Later, I was sorry to see its perfection marred, when, try as I might to cut it neatly, I'd ruin its perfect roundedness. My greed was tinged with sadness. It was a similar feeling when Ma put plantain still dripping with palm oil in front of me. Despite my fascination with their golden beauty came a sense of inevitability, for I knew their fleshy flavour would soon be defiled.

The feeling persisted for a long time. I am still sad whenever I call to mind the bright, fleeting images of those moments spent with the stranger who had taken my mother's place. Ma's image was as familiar as that of my relations; she had been that peaceful old lady with jet-black eyes.

▼

I would drift into a dream whenever my eyes fell upon her papaya-fragile silhouette.

There were nights, as I touched the bamboo bed where I knew Ma's body had lain in the dip in the mattress, when it seemed I was touching death itself, and I clung to the hope that the brilliance of the light of the sun would not delay its going down. Little by little my grief was receding until, in a final spurt, it was swallowed up by the dark absence in which I languished, my eyes fixed like a child's on the dragonfly he wants to catch, on this invisible mother of mine.

Today, the inventory brings her back, and however much I tell myself I must be mad or obsessed with an absurd desire to see surface within me the monsters I believed were there although I couldn't name or identify them, I can't help wondering whether my image-filled eyes aren't hiding Ma's face bathed in the light of the setting sun.

My heart has become so fragile. A bird sings in the wood through which I'm wandering. I walk in the shade, pick up the yellow leaf that falls at my feet, and kiss it. A memory comes flooding back: the inexplicable thrill at the sight of the leaf outside Ma's hut was warranted and explained why for so long I was rapt with wonder by the birdsong that I thought I was hearing for the first time.

These strange notions, the yellow leaves, were surely in me. I hadn't paid them much attention before – they had probably developed, and the memory of the birdsong wouldn't have affected me so much had it not reminded me of the song of the two woodpigeons.

Everything in the world has changed and everything in me has changed. Sometimes I think all I have to do is leave myself open to experiences I would previously have rejected, because I feel more exposed and less vulnerable.

I look for signs, and while the moan of a sweet-smelling breeze can remind me of Ma's absence, it also stirs a strange desire in me for her absence to be mine too. I wish that absence could annihilate me completely, since it took from me the only being I had ever loved.

33: The Revelation

▼

It was a long time coming and, try as I might with each trip I made to anticipate it, I didn't think the day would ever come when I finally understood why Ma had disappeared.

There had been signs, ambiguous signs that had taken a long time to decipher, urging me to go and see old Ada, a childhood friend of Ma's. It is said that Ada had seen the day born and night disappear.

When I arrived at the old, shrivelled, black hut, Ada sat me down among his chickens and guinea pigs and told me all about Mamie Titi's life and her mysterious relationship with Father Delanoé. He told me that each was as bad as the other when it came to being obsessed with the hereafter. Did he believe he had solved the mystery of Ma?

The old man's story was very disturbing.

'You see, Ékéla, every morning she'd go into the forest looking for herbs. Her whole beauty was concentrated in eyes that could delight anybody they touched and with it, their soul. This vision might just have been an exquisite echo of the way I felt whenever I saw her. But not only did the image engage the senses, it also called for a transformation of the self, a complete metamorphosis of one's perceptions. She instilled the world with a new essence. Her voice took over the visible, and from out of her mouth came a double-edged sword that told you not to sacrifice to idols.'

Perturbed, old Ada resumed, 'It was as if she had the power to breathe life into nature and make it speak. Mamie Titi's voice could bring down the rain; her smile could open the sky and breach the silence of the gods.

'Suffused with night's scents, spilled before they could be captured, she'd sit at the foot of the coconut palm, and as she garnered splashes of sunlight and rocked with happiness, she'd say, "Try as I might to hold onto them, they always escape me."

'Ékéla, I'd have sworn she was trying to collect the scattered substances that elude the senses. Only at dusk would she finally speak.

'They came from every tribe, every nation, every language to hear her. When they were with her, they felt no hunger, no thirst and the heat of the fire did not burn them. Plunged into darkness, they were able to suspend body and mind, intoxicated on words sweet to their ears though they spawned bitterness in their bellies. And whilst the words tormented their souls, their eyes opened the sky so the rain could fall once the oracle had spoken.

'As she spoke their four truths, their hearts closed over an unspeakable grief. In an excess of pain, they bit their tongues as they felt something that they strained to see. Their souls joined as she cleansed them of all malice.

'One night,' Ada went on, his eyes brimming with tears, 'she spotted a man in the crowd and chose him. She decided that in front of everyone she would open his eyes so that he could access the invisible world and see what others do not. Excluded from the collective consciousness, the man felt dispossessed. He couldn't understand how such a woman could be willing to share her powers. He prostrated himself and wept. Ashamed that she'd exposed his weakness, he spoke at length as on a Whitsunday morning. The knot of his destiny had been securely tied.

'He saw draw near the end of both sadness and joy, that no sadness or joy could measure. He knew he was destined for higher things and surrendered to the superior will that towered over him, pointing to a greater desire.

'When Mamie Titi blew on his eyes, he was conscious of a universal conflagration of which his body was the incombustible centre.

'It was dreadful. We heard a noise like rushing water, the crash of thunder, the crackle of a distant fire. The River Ewoé was drying up and surrendering the dead enshrouded in its waters. The forest turned into the purest of golds. Then the man said, "You are day, you are night, the beginning of all beginnings of the word."

'Transfixed by pain and adoration, the man was struck by lightning. Mamie Titi had bestowed on him two extra eyes. He saw the souls of those whose heads had been cut off, he saw the waters rise from their beds, he saw a burning bush from which a voice rose. In each man he now perceived a knot of violence.

'All the phantasmagorias of night and day, that make up the whole universe, displayed, as though reflected in a celestial mirror, an aura of pleasure. His staring eyes were fixed on a complete and remarkable reality that had plunged him into the beginnings of knowledge, the love of origins and the scent of death.

'Much later,' Ada observed, 'the man understood that what had predestined him thus was his capacity for hope and his aptitude for solitude. He realised Mamie Titi had given him everything; that she'd given herself to him so that he would see and so that, like her, he would open the eyes of those who do not see.

'No one understood how Mamie Titi could have chosen a foreigner, a white man to succeed her.'

Ada sobbed as he described the violence that raged over the whole country. 'The firestorm roared, tribe attacked tribe, nations split and men killed one another in an inexplicable frenzy. A chaotic and overflowing spring of hatred had been let loose.

'For a long time,' he said, 'the men gathered outside, waited for the return of she who loosened tongues. An atmosphere of fear and longing prevailed, intensified by the overpowering absence of Mamie Titi.

'Her oracular words lingered in memories. Long after her disappearance, the way she intoned her prophesies still punctuated conversations, the shadow of her fingers as they disclosed their secrets during the laying on of hands, still inspired blind devotion. Their orphaned thoughts discovered the tribulation of abandonment, the sear of a grace that touches the tongue and reduces it to a stammer.

'Prisoners of an infernal Babel, the men droned. Shrouded in night's veils, they raised their eyes when they heard a voice from beyond the mists of the setting sun, which, before it could brush against their faces, they knew for certain would live on in them, would never know death, and that everything in their memories would protect its mark, and that nothing in their futures would betray its memory.

'They felt in her renunciation that she had left them and savoured the pleasure of sacrificing even her name.

'Mamie Titi's goodness had kept her in this ideal and abstract existence, had bid her live on in these particular eternal circumstances and arouse an insatiable desire for a now invisible and perfect presence through a face fallen silent.

'It was then,' continued a stunned Ada, 'that two woodpigeons who spoke the language of men passed through the night. The fire of their shadows grazed the tops of the coconut palms. The stars lacked lustre. Suddenly, the mountain shook and the hills trembled. Nature burst into flames and everything around died. Even the skies folded and curled like a book.

'You might find it hard to believe, Ékéla,' said Ada, 'but all the men fell to their knees like leaves falling from the vine or fig. And just as in the Apocalypse, arid land became a lake, and the parched earth a fountain. We thought we spied a woman gathering the tears of the gods. In the lairs of wild animals, we saw the green shoots of reeds and rushes come to life.

'When nothing was left of the ancient past, and following the collapse of the sky and the destruction of things, for a long time all that remained was memory and the glare of truth to witness, to await, to hope for, among the ruins of a bruised earth, the coming of the woman in mourning for the world.

'Only then,' concluded Ada, 'did the men understand that Mamie Titi had left them for good, that she had sacrificed herself to pass on her powers to a white man. On the sacred track she used to take, they made a bed of bracken and laid a lily there.'

A white man! So it was Father Delanoé. By accepting the gift of Ma's powers, he had killed her. It was he I'd seen at Ma's side in my *eboka* dream.

It seemed to me that my whole life had concealed

itself in the discovery of this hatred. I, Sabeth, was no more than a great void around this unforgivable murder.

Unconsoled, I would always keep the wound open. What I must therefore question again, is neither the reality nor the depth of my hatred; it is whether or not I have once again made a mistake, whether or not I am desperate to hide from the truth and why.

34: Ma's Grave

▼

I felt a need to clarify Father Delanoé's role in relation to Ma.

The day I went to consult Father Delanoé, I had noticed scattered on the ground, the lower branches of palm trees and white curtains at the windows while conventuals usually lived their suspended, half-frozen, ceremonial lives devoted to God.

That day, I couldn't help wondering whether the Father hadn't taken his place in the hieratic procession of African witchdoctors, whether the whiteness of his skin hadn't cleansed him of the invisible covering of secrets that required a candle be there not to give light but to enlighten.

Father Delanoé wasn't African, yet there was something about him, something indiscernible, and unknown to me, that bore out his occult powers, just as being in the water can turn a tree trunk into a crocodile.

And yet, however strong the traditional practitioner's powers might have been, I viewed him with growing suspicion. There had been signs, clues that the recollection of the Father lifting the curse from me had, as though by a miracle, erased. But he no longer has a strange hold over me and I can no longer turn a blind eye. I remember my uncertainty, my flinching, my sense of outrage – there's no other word for it – when the Father turned down Ma's invitation to a meal the day following their last meeting.

And should I not feel, before it disappears completely, and even though it was ostensibly an insignificant event, my heart thump, a painful emptiness, a stab of jealousy at the thought of the initiation rite that had united Ma and the Father, and which the mother of witchdoctors had refused to allow me to witness?

Since no animal was sacrificed to seal the rite, a human being would find death there.

What masks my irritation or hatred of the Father is the strength of the twelve-year bond between Mamie Titi and her disciple, and the long, now broken attachment that endures despite all the vicissitudes that led to Ma's sacrifice so that he could outlive her.

Hence I confess my despair. Sobbing tears of anguish I sway, as everything I try to hang on to forsakes me, and as I remember the kiss Ma gave Father Delanoé, kiss passed on breath to breath.

My innate faithfulness to truth made me listen to old Ada who had seen the day being born and night disappear, as though there might be another truth, just as dangerous, being relayed by the gossips of Douala and Yaoundé; but before I could reach it I'd have to push back the relentless screen of lies that was prompting me to reject my own truth.

Father Delanoé would only have become a witchdoctor when Mamie Titi opened his eyes at the climax of the initiation; and as she passed her powers on to him, she opened her own eyes on death. No transfer of power is immediate. There is always, at the last moment, an extra wait, the final test, the selection or acceptance of finitude.

I could picture Ma and the coconut palm where she liked to officiate, but all she would have given me again was a whisper charged with emotion, her birdbone flute, the memory of the lyrebird, the two woodpigeons, the inner mystery I strive desperately to bring into the world.

Immortal, all-powerful, oblivious to the demands of a body that crumbles, that finds refuge in sleep, Ma would continue, for all eternity, to watch over the dead and the living.

So that nothing of the world where she had breathed would ever be altered or defiled, or because Father Delanoé observed alone the places and objects that spoke to him without returning the gaze that had so often fallen on them, Ma had made me her daughter, gauging the feeling that connected us, kindling the pain of having been born the daughter of truth.

About Ma, my mother, I would have liked to know everything. Being close to Ma, I had the impression there was an abiding hurt she didn't want me to know about, some atavistic shame she had wanted to protect me from in case I became contaminated. She probably never admitted, not even to herself, how not having brought a child into the world had left her free from care.

Never had I been so aware of my pain, my wound, but rather than guiding me to the ravaged shore I was gradually making my way towards, they ended up leading me to the joy of a new filiation.

Ma was dead. And at last I understood that music alone could free me from the song which was wearing me, her daughter, down to the point of exhaustion. Finally I was able to feel the thrill that the two woodpigeons' song had forced into me.

But for the present, I was but a gaping wound, appeased in absence, cast alive into the same abyss, the same grave. In memory of Ma.

35: The Annunciation

The smallest of lives began to surface in my memory, ready to overrun me and block out the world. I remembered the Sénoufo mask I'd seen in Father Delanoé's oratory. I loved the fear-provoking language, the timeless images of the sacred – coagulation of blackened wood, antelope horn, skin, brass and cowrie hair.

These days I'm intrigued by how the language of knowledge takes images from the earth, from nature and from the animal and vegetal kingdoms. I had been cut off from these, but Ma had reconnected me with them.

My whole life flashed before my eyes like an emotional outburst; with it came the same tension, the same nervous apprehension, unbearable and blinding like the shaft of light that had just dazzled me.

When I discovered I was pregnant again, that a new life was growing inside me, I knew I wouldn't disappear without forcing out into the world the searing pain I had carried within me since childhood.

Whatever happened, I knew my life would continue to expand outside me, that inside me another life was already protracting my existence, and that it was from me that this life would take its shape. Thanks to this new hope, I might now be able to live with my husband, like other women, a life that would never be completely mine.

To me, to my parents, Obala had always been a haven, a refuge. When I had dreamed of marrying Emmanuel and probably when I was given to my husband too, it was that same sense of security I was after.

Today, I am as far away from it as I was when I was a young child filled with self-doubt, when something thwarted this great need of mine to take hold of the world and tame it.

I had lived, at least ostensibly; I'd founded a family, had a child that tradition had taken from me, and whose absence I had for so long found difficult to accept. Maybe I'd only ever lived in a dream, the way I'd lived trancelike around a face, around Emmanuel's love, the way I'd been held back, damaged by the very relationships I longed to have with people, and maybe that was how I would eventually find myself again.

All the time I had believed I could be free, or tried to be free, I had only been deluding myself.

Perhaps motherhood, which had brought me nothing but pain and anxiety, would now be the citadel, the refuge that my mother and I, and all women before us, had expectantly though vainly sought in the past, but never in the present.

The resurrection; barely had the new light risen from the ruins of love and begun to shine, than it dazzled and filled me with joy. My eyes on the child to come – I knew it would be a girl – my beacon, I stopped stumbling and was able at last to make my way towards the light.

Would I be worthy of her enthusiasms, her burning passion, of the impulse, which, since I'd been given to my husband, had striven to destroy and give life? An existence depended on this imminent birth! What catalyst was developing inside me, what as yet unknown future was it endeavouring to shape in the dark?

Dusk would soon cover the trees with peace. I had been leaning on a nonexistent pillar, on a fraught and dispirited passion that had in all probability brought Emmanuel and me together in a similar unprofessed panic.

So that I might increase the pasturelands of my heart, so that I might accept the respite I was being offered, so that I might breathe a while longer, I had to accept my life and all its shortcomings.

The bright promise of the child to come pulled me from my old darkness, delineated its strength, its remarkable glow. With each day that passed I became more convinced I was carrying a girl. The one we dream of, even before it is born, is the one we shall love.

I couldn't possibly carry another son after Douo, replace the child who'd been stolen from me and stifle the howl of desperation that still makes me shudder.

There are times when I am troubled by the presence of the child to come as well as imbued with her sweetness; when, filled with awe, I am one with the golden breath of her silent breathing. I emerge screaming from this honey nimbus, receptive through all of my fissures to the most intense, most destructive of experiences, which, rather than close up, I enlarge so that, my back to the night, I might feel more wounded, more exposed, and better able to nourish the child inside me.

Devastating purity of love and renunciation that fractures or lights the soul, rekindled glow of the mirage, bliss more searing than a blazing inferno, my daughter will be called Sylvie. The wild one.

Return to the shadows all the memories that might still want to haunt me, and may I never yearn to remove or raise the seal placed over oblivion. Return to the shadows the image of the firstborn taken from me – for it feels as if something from which I might never recover is secretly moving around inside me. A new bond is about to be formed that will never be broken.

Suffused in, absorbing, reflecting the glow of joy, of motherhood, of my future daughter's eyes dotted with shifting gold specks, I accept all the lives emotion has forced on me, so that they might remain inside me like a book one unfolds; all the lives offered me, onto which I shall open my eyes.

36: The Birth

▼

I see it on Yaoundé's seven shimmering hills, on the sprawling River Ewoé, on the palm trees, on the wings of the hummingbird. It heightens everything, it is all I see, this blissful feeling, which sucks me up out of myself. It is etched in my mind, it leads me far from the solitary sisal, far from the ache that prevents me from completely dissolving into the child to come.

On this trembling morning of 21 March, I leave the house and go out. The last of the dry season's heat has exhausted me. My *kaba* sticks to my protruding belly. I am short of breath and it hurts to breathe as I walk awkwardly, urged on by the restless crushing weight. A quiet fountain intermingled with the heady smell of roots and upturned seaweed flows down my thighs.

Struck by dawn's extreme limpidity that takes my breath away, I know at twenty-one what childbirth is and know my time is near. I tremble with joy, amazed that I feel no pain.

As a screeching whirlwind of woodpigeons soars up and dawn is torn by the pink and grey wings, my womb shudders and distends; I feel the pressure tear it apart and my flesh in upheaval.

I lie on the damp red earth between the well and a clump of peonies. My body relaxes, steeped in the miracle that is taking place. I feel the bones between my hips and vertebrae part; I hear them move with ease, widening and opening, as though there dwelt inside me a persistent, tortured and shrill song. The chords rise from my wide-open mouth and fall to my belly where I reach for what is gently, so very gently emerging.

As I feel the child's body slide from me, a blinding spasm has me cry out in pain. It is then that I understand that the child whose cord that binds it to the bowels of the earth has not been cut, was inside me. Overwhelmed with sensations and visions, I am amazed at the dense existence of the supernatural that planted the proof of Soulé's prophesy in my womb. Then Father Delanoé's words come back to me: 'The truth lies within you. You wouldn't be searching for it if you hadn't already found it.'

And now I cut the cord so that Sylvie can come into the world, so that she can fulfil her destiny as a woman.

As I am reborn into the world, the women rush from the house to wrap me in damp cloths, and with their winks and compliments, they welcome the new little girl, over whom I shed nine tears of joy. While some attend to me, others hold the child high and chant, 'Three cheers for the mother! Hip, hip hurray! Hip, hip hurray! Hip, hip hurray!'

With each new emotion comes a new revelation, each time more staggering, until finally I remember Ma's memorable words, 'The second a child comes into the world, an angel slaps him in the face to make him forget the joy of being in his mother's womb; nothing is left of this bliss, not even in the remnants of dreams that sometimes surface. Forgetfulness finally prevails, creating the groove on the child's upper lip as he's hurled into the world.'

No words can now bring back the echo of the paradise lost, the inner rhythm that prefigures forms, except perhaps the thrill of the bird-bone flute that had exploded in my face and whose mystery was alive in the newborn baby.

I turn and look at Sylvie, the wild one, and tell her never to let silence have the last word, never to forget the song of the two woodpigeons. I tell myself the same thing and instantly hope engulfs me, bearing me away as I am propelled into the light.

Other BlackAmber titles:

All that Blue
Gaston-Paul Effa

Ancestors
Paul Crooks

Nothing But The Truth
Mark Wray

Paddy Indian
Cauvery Madhavan

Ordinary Lives
– Extraordinary Women
Joan Blaney

The Holy Woman
Qaisra Shahraz

What Goes Around
Sylvester Young

Brixton Rock
Alex Wheatle

One Bright Child
Patricia Cumper

CHARTERHOUSE LIBRARY
019681